Twisted
KNIGHT

Green Hills Academy Trilogy

Book 2

Josie Max

TWISTED KNIGHT

For information contact :
Josie Max at josiemax@josiemaxwrites.com
http://www.josiemaxwrites.com

Cover design by Josie Max
ISBN: 978-1-955184-01-4

First Edition: March 2021

978-1-955184-01-4

CONTENTS

PROLOGUE

Violet

"YOU KNOW I LOVE YOU, right?" My mom's emerald eyes glistened with unshed tears as she fiddled with the locket around her neck.

I sat up from our worn, brown plaid

couch. "Is something wrong?" An unease settled on my shoulders, something I hadn't felt in almost a year.

She had been acting strange ever since I came home from school. One second, she was excited to be getting her one-year chip from Narcotics Anonymous on Sunday. The next, she would stare at me with worry lining her eyes.

That was typical behavior for my mom before she got clean. But now, it had me worried.

Her smile was brittle. "No. I don't say it enough. Maybe since I'm hitting one year sober it's made me a little misty-eyed." She shrugged.

I waved her to the couch, hoping what she said was true. The sofa wasn't big—just big enough for us—but it was ours.

Even her footsteps felt hesitant, but she made her way over and sat with a loud sigh.

I shifted to face her. “Spill it.”

Was I holding on to lingering anger from her drug days? Yes. But as my aunt Dahlia reminded me, she was my mom. She loved me, and she was trying.

Therefore, I’d try too. If she was about to admit to using again, I’d listen. I’d be crying on the inside, but I’d be there for her as she revealed to me what I feared.

She bit her lip. “Have you ever . . . Nothing. Never mind.”

I brushed my mom’s smooth dark brown hair behind her ear. “Have I ever what?”

She adjusted herself on the couch until her eyes lifted to mine. “I love you with all my heart.”

I nodded. “Yes, we’ve established that.”

“Of course.” She smiled. “I guess I should just come out and ask. Have you ever wondered about your father?"

My head reared back. That was the last question I would expect her to ask.

I nibbled my lower lip, grateful she wasn't considering doing drugs again, but upset that she waited all this time to bring up my father.

She never said a word about the man. When I was young, I thought he was an alien from another planet and that one day he would beam me up to his spaceship. That was how little I knew about him.

And when I asked, she'd warn me it was best that I never knew.

"Yes. What kid growing up fatherless wouldn't want to know?"

She took my hand in hers. It was warm and weathered, but there was comfort in her touch.

"There's a reason I haven't told you about him. Not that I didn't want to tell you. It's just . . ."

My mom stared at our hands, and that was when the thought entered my head. Something so obvious that I felt like an idiot I hadn't thought of it before. It would explain so much.

"He, uh . . . he didn't hurt you, did he?"

Her head popped up with eyes like saucers. "No. Oh, goodness, no."

I tilted my head. "Then what? What could have kept you from telling me about my father?"

"It's very complicated. When I met your father, he was a different person." She gave me an unusual grin.

The look on her face was an expression I had never seen before. Serene. Blissful. Someone who was in love.

"So, you dated?"

"Yes. He was sweet and so romantic. Not at all like me." My mother giggled.

That man obviously made her happy. Why had she kept that from me?

"Okay. And?"

I wanted her to continue. She was showing me such a different side of herself. Normally, she worried about bills or was exhausted from working two jobs.

When she mentioned my father, it was like the years had slipped away from her face.

"And you have his eyes . . .. Those dark, honey-brown eyes look just like his. Even the shape."

I lifted my fingers to the corners of my eyes. It felt good to know more about me and where I came from. It was comforting.

"And your sass." She snorted while pursing her lips. "Your father knew what he wanted, and when people questioned him, he knew exactly what buttons to push. Just like you, little lady." My mom pointed at me.

"But why haven't you told me any of this before?"

Her carefree expression faded, and the unease settled back into place.

"It's not just about him. If he had his way, he would have happily been in your life. But where he's from, it doesn't work like that." Her fingers slipped from mine as she settled further into the couch.

"Is he from another country?" The more she told me, the more questions I had.

"No. He was from here."

My eyes widened. "South Green Hills Trailer Park?"

"No, from Green Hills. North Green Hills to be exact."

I gasped. That was where all the richies lived. The millionaires and billionaires and all other *'aires* I couldn't count.

"So, he has money?"

She covered her eyes with her arm and leaned her head back. "*Had.* Had money. That's not why I wanted to talk to you about him, Violet. That's not important."

"Are you serious?" I yelped while waving my hand around. "Look where we live, Mom. I'm thankful for all we have, but to say we don't struggle is a lie. Some money, any money would help. At any point when I was growing up we could have used some of that 'not so important' money."

My mom sat up, dropping her arm. "This is why I didn't want to tell you about him—"

I stood. "What? You're the reason I know nothing about my father? All this time I thought he was the one. That he ran away when he found out you were pregnant or was in jail or something bad.

But it was *you* who wanted to keep secret the fact that he could easily have given us a few days' worth of salary to help feed us for a year."

She stood, trying to reach for me, but I shrugged her off. "No, you don't get to do that. I turn eighteen later this year, and I am just now finding out about my dad. A man who wanted to be in my life, but my mother prevented it."

"That's not true. You're upset, Violet . . . as you should be. But like I said, it's complicated. It's not that I didn't want you to know your dad or that he had money; it's that if you found out . . . let me just say, there are people who wouldn't be so welcoming to you. I did it to protect you."

I looked away and folded my arms. "It's obvious you will not tell me the truth."

With anger and disappointment being beaten out by my heart, I slid my eyes to my mother. She was predictable in many ways—like how she danced around touchy subjects.

When she brought up my father, I was hopeful to finally know more about him. But I should have known better. The most I got out of her was the color of his eyes.

"Are you even going to tell me his name?"

"It's getting late. Why don't I make you Grandma's tea to help you rest?"

I knew it. Not even a name.

"Fine." There was no point to keep asking. She would say nothing.

I watched her putter around our tiny kitchenette in our trailer. She took the old, blackened tea kettle and placed it on the stove.

"I don't know why you even bothered to bring him up if you weren't going to tell me much of anything about him," I mumbled.

The sigh from my mom was loud, but she kept on making the tea.

After a moment, she shuffled over with steam floating up from a red mug.

"Here. Drink this, then head to bed." She handed over the hot tea.

I took a sip and winced. "I don't remember the tea being this bitter."

My mother's eyes fluttered to the floor. "It's been a while since you've had it. The tea's always been a little bitter. But it helps you get a good night's rest."

The last time I had it was when I was a kid, sick with the flu.

I sipped the tea while my mother busied herself tidying up the kitchen and living area. There wasn't much to clean, but that never stopped her from fussing about the place being a mess.

Once I gulped down the last drop, I put

the cup in the sink and yawned.

"I'm heading to bed, Mom," I said without looking at her.

Was I still mad at her for keeping all the things she knew about my dad from me? Absolutely. But she was my mom, and we lived together in a very tiny trailer. I had to suck it up.

"Good night, Violet. And remember, I love you with all my heart."

I nodded and headed toward the back.

"Violet," my mom called when I got to the bedroom door.

"Yes?"

"His name was Jack. And I promise to tell you everything tomorrow, okay?"

A smile erupted on my face. I ran over and gave her a tight squeeze.

"Thank you." I pulled back and gazed into her beautiful green eyes. I had always been jealous of the color, but now that I knew my dad had brown eyes too, I wasn't so envious anymore.

"Go to bed." She patted my shoulder.

I sighed and walked lazily to my bed, grabbing my worn smiley face T-shirt and jammie pants to change into. I didn't even care that the pants had a hole in the knee. I was too excited about all that I would learn in the morning.

ONE

Violet

Six Months Later

"**What are you in** here for? Let me guess, trying to score a dime bag off a nark, little girl?" The woman's dark eyes narrowed as I studied the black tattoo that snaked down her neck and under her black T-shirt.

I wiggled my tongue in the space of my missing tooth. Since the bus accident, I hadn't had time to go to the dentist to get it fixed. Luckily, it was toward the back of my mouth, and no one could tell.

I had been in this jail cell for the last three hours waiting for my phone call. But who would I call? My aunt? She now lived under Knight's roof.

I was so fucked.

"I'm talking to you, little girl." She stood from her corner, running her hands through her long black hair after it fell in her face. She continued to walk over to me before she stopped to hover.

I knew a girl just like her back at South Green Hills. She acted tough and tatted up, just like the woman standing over me now.

Her name was Janice. And one day Janice picked on the wrong kid. That kid called her bluff, fought back, and Janice deflated like a hot-air balloon. Shrank into nothing.

I picked at my nail, never letting the woman above me notice the worry in my eyes.

"No, not drugs."

There was a shove to my arm, and I winced. The pain from what happened in the bus accident spiked up my arm.

"Come on, bitch. Or are you too scared?" she mocked in a childish tone.

She was tall but lanky. So skinny, I was sure Seraphina and her bitch crew would be jealous.

I thought for sure it was Seraphina who made up the story I killed John Lenker. But the way Knight said bye to me as I was arrested made me realize that he did it.

"I'm not scared." I stood and pushed myself into her body, startling her. Apparently, she hadn't expected that.

Perhaps she would hit me and try to take me down. With my clavicle fracture, she could do it. That would not stop me from standing up for myself though.

Her nostrils flared, and I could tell she wouldn't back down. There were too many witnesses to her madness. Three other women sat in the cell, waiting for the show. In here, like back in my old school, saving face was more important than physical pain.

"Stop frontin', Drew," a voice called from behind.

I glanced over to discover a tall woman about my aunt's age, with sharp gray eyes and red hair. At least, I thought it was red. There wasn't much there as it was shaved down like a buzz cut.

Drew turned. "Seriously, Jewel?"

Jewel narrowed her eyes. "Did I stutter?"

Drew shook her head and moved back to the bench in the corner on the opposite end of the cell.

I nodded to Jewel, silently thanking her. I may not have been in jail before, but I knew enough from people I grew up with to realize silence was golden.

Jewel's eyes slid over my body, and something about the way she watched me caused my blood to turn cold.

"You don't look like a murderer to me," Jewel said as smoothly as if she were asking me where I got my shoes.

I straightened my back. "I never said I was in here for murder—"

"Please." She held up her hand. "There ain't much I don't know around here. You go to that stuck-up school on the north side of town."

My heart thudded in my chest.

What else did she know about me? And who

told her?

She stood from the bench and sashayed over as if this holding cell was her palace and I was the banquet set out for her to feast on.

My eyes darted around the cell. They all locked gazes on me. Were they about to pounce too?

I wasn't scared of Drew, but I was wholeheartedly freaked out by Jewel. It was always the people who barely had to lift a finger that I feared the most. The ones who blustered around and made threats were nothing. But Jewel was like a deadly snake, and I had stupidly meandered right into her path.

When she stood next to me, she slid her arm over my shoulders. It hurt when hand rested right on the broken part near my shoulder, but my face was stone. I didn't dare bat an eye.

"I just started going to North Green Hills a month ago. Before that, I lived on the South Side."

As if that would help my case. The fact that I had stepped foot into North Green Hills put a target on my back. I didn't even look at Jewel; I knew she didn't care.

"How'd that happen?" She pointed to my arm in a sling.

"Bus accident. It went down the side of a mountain."

She gasped and took a step back, letting her arm fall from my shoulder. Relief flooded my body as the pain eased.

"No shit. Damn, that's some fucked-up shit." She shook her head. "You know, my cousin drives buses."

I nodded. "Yeah?"

She ran her fingers through her almost non-existent hair. "He's a nice guy. Trying to be a good guy. Have a proper job, shit like that. And the strange thing is he told me about how a bus he drove went off the side of a mountain too."

My eyes widened. "What?"

She nodded. "Yeah, I asked how he suddenly got a brand-new car and bought a brand-new phone. It's not like bus drivers make bank, ya know." She rolled her eyes. "Anyway, he told me that some blond bimbo paid him lots of money to be away from the bus for a while."

It must have been Seraphina. As memories of that day came back to me, I wondered if she had a hand in it. The fight we had on the bus and when her friends kept looking around outside as if they were waiting for something. It was all so weird.

"That was it? She paid him to stay away?"

Her lips curled. "That wasn't

everything. But if you want to know more, you've got to pay."

My eyebrows rose. "I don't have money. The only reason I'm going to Green Hills Academy is because the creepy mayor felt sorry for me after my mom died and paid for me to go there. If she hadn't died at Happy Pond, I would still be at South Green Hills High."

She tilted her head. "Wait, was your mom Rose Adler?"

"Oh man, I heard about what happened during the spring. That was crazy," Drew piped up.

I rubbed my brow. "Yup. That was my mom. And before you ask, I don't remember what happened. Apparently, she drugged me so I slept through the whole thing."

Jewel glanced over at the other women in the cell and waved them off. I had no idea where they could go because the place was tiny, but they all went to huddle in a corner together.

She came over to me and leaned in. "Look, I used to know Rose. We, uh . . . used to sell together, ya know?"

I shook my head.

Jewel blew out a breath. "Deal. We both started dealing elicit a few years ago. But she got out last year. I don't blame her. That shit is terrible. Something is wrong with it. I stopped selling it too, but sometimes . . . well, ya know, I got to make some cash. And it pays." She shrugged sheepishly.

Where we both were from, doing things you hated was just part of everyday life. On the South Side, there was no room for morals; it was all about survival.

I wasn't okay with her selling it because I had heard about that drug. A few kids I went to school with back on the South Side OD'd on it.

But I didn't hate her. I felt sorry for her and realized how lucky I had it. Yeah, my mom died, and what had happened to me over the past month and a half was terrible, but I never had to resort to that shit to survive.

"I didn't realize my mom sold it."

"For a while. She never used it, okay. Just know that. Rose was a good woman, but she did other stuff. Other drugs. And addiction can make you do stupid shit, kid. It's like you turn into a robot, with only one thing you were designed to do, and you will do whatever it takes to make it happen."

I frowned. I used to wonder why my mom chose drugs over me for years. When I was younger, it hurt. She had broken my heart. But the way Jewel was talking, it made sense. I remember all too well that glazed look in my mom's eyes when all she wanted was to get high. Nothing I said or did would stop her.

"I just wish I could have reprogrammed her, if you know what I mean."

Jewel sighed. "Yeah, I get it. That's why I don't do it." She puffed out her chest as if dealing was better than using. It wasn't. In my mind, it was worse.

"So, you were better than my mom?" I narrowed my eyes as I watched her frown.

"No, I'm not. It's fucked-up, but I have a kid at home too. What job could I get?" She stepped back and waved a hand around her neck, showing all her tats.

"Look, I don't know you, but you knew my mom. You say you know things. I don't think my mom OD'd because she went on a bender. I think someone drugged her and killed her."

I had kept that to myself for so long. It felt good to let it out, even if she was a stranger.

Jewel nodded, letting my words sink in.

I heard keys jingling and glanced over as a shadow grew on the floor. Someone was coming.

"I can't help you in here, but do you know where Benny's Tattoo Parlor is over on Delta Road?"

The door opened, and Officer Harris stared at me. "It seems someone posted bail for you, Ms. Adler. Come with me."

My eyes widened. "Who?"

The officer shrugged. "I don't know. The girl you were with when I arrested you."

Arabella? I never knew she'd put up with that kind of money. When I found out the bail the judge set for me an hour ago was over a hundred grand, I thought I was never getting out.

"Don't forget what I said. Benny's," Jewel murmured as I strolled out of the cell.

I gave her a nod before going down the hall and out the door to the main part of the police station. It took a few minutes until I got to see Arabella because I had to sign some paperwork. But once I stepped out to the front of the precinct, I ran over and gave her a hug.

"Thank you so much," I mumbled into her shoulder, trying to muzzle my wobbly voice.

"Don't thank me," Arabella said as she pulled away. "Thank Knight."

I frowned. "For getting me arrested? Not on your life."

She furrowed her brows. "If he got you arrested, then why did he give me the money to bail you out?"

TWO

Knight

"IF YOUR UNCLE SAW me coming here . . ." Edwin Locklear said as his eyes scanned the room.

I let him wallow in unease for a little while longer. That uncertainty would help me. Anything I said to appease his fears, he'd gobble up. People were funny like that, so easily duped.

A small drop of empathy mixed with a few kind words and they were hooked.

"I get it." I held up my hands and leaned back in what was once my uncle's home office chair. "And don't you worry. I have spies everywhere. You're just one of many. I know where that man is at all times."

I went on a spending spree once I came into my inheritance on my eighteenth birthday. Hiring detectives and paying people to monitor the mayor for me were my first purchases.

He studied me for a moment, but I kept my features neutral. "Aren't you supposed to be in school? You're only eighteen."

He was right. If I were a forty-something-year-old man and worked my way up the ladder dealing with people who didn't always follow the rules to gain success, I'd be suspicious of a teenager too.

But I wasn't like most teenagers.

"School is closed today. There was a death there. It will be closed for the week."

He nodded. "Yeah, I heard what happened. And they're saying one student did it."

I closed my eyes and inhaled. When I opened them again, I gave a hard smile. "Something like that. I suppose the police will find the killer. It's their job."

"Right," he said with a sigh. "The file I gave you on the memory stick is all I could get from Mr. King."

"Do you think he suspects that his own assistant is stealing information from him and giving it to me?"

"No. At least, I don't think so. He hasn't

said or done anything to give that impression. And it's been business as usual since he came back from overseas. Typical mayoral stuff."

My eyes slid to the memory stick he put on the desk when he first arrived ten minutes ago. The contrast of the teal blue against the dark grain of wood from the old-style desk made the stick pop. Much like the contrast between me and my uncle.

"He hasn't met with anyone unusual or had any private calls with anyone he didn't want you to know about?"

"Not really. He had lunch with Kiki the other day. Right after he came back from his trip."

I shrugged. "Why would that be unusual? Kiki is his wife."

Edwin's lips thinned. "Come on, Knight. Even you know their marriage is a sham. She gets money, and he gets eye candy on his arm. It's a contract, nothing more."

"That's true. But I've seen them have dinner at the house together many times."

His brows rose. "Did you have dinner with them?"

"No. Ava and I always ate in the kitchen with the staff."

He pointed his finger at me as if it were a gun. "Exactly. It's rare for Ichabod to have a meal with Kiki. Or do anything with her. But when it happens, it's always private."

I rubbed my chin. He was right. I rarely saw them together. If they were in the same room, they were doing separate things. He would be on his cell, and she'd be on her laptop. Not even a greeting passed between them.

"Try to find out what they met about.

I'll do some digging on my end."

"That will not be easy, Knight. It's not like I record their meetings."

I smirked. "I wouldn't be so sure of that."

Earlier this year, I was positive my uncle was making plans to officially adopt Ava and take control of her money. I bugged his office, both here and at his job.

He held up his hands. "Whatever you're doing, I don't want to know about it. I'm already nervous enough taking these files and giving them to you. If he finds out . . . who knows what will happen."

"My uncle knows I have other information that, if it got out, he'd be fucked." My thoughts drifted back to what he and his buddies tried to do to Violet in the pool house. "I doubt he's going to do anything that would make it worse for him."

Edwin stood and shook his head. "That's easy for you to say. Look at where you live." He waved at the giant marble-framed fireplace and vaulted ceiling. "You've got money. You and your uncle have always had money and access to people who can protect you. I grew up on the South Side. I have no one to help me if I get in trouble. I don't know if I can do this anymore."

He made his way to the sliding double doors. I got up and jogged over to catch him before he left.

"You're right. I can't relate. I was born with a silver spoon in my mouth. But if you think I have people to protect me, you're wrong. I don't care what happens to me. If my uncle wanted to chop me up into little bits and feed me to the sharks, that's fine. But I need to protect my sister. I'm all she has. And to protect her, I need to know what Ichabod King is up to. Why isn't he running for re-election? Why the daily press conferences about the jobs he's bringing to town?"

"Franklin First Laboratories is expanding. The mayor worked out a deal with the board of Franklin First to open it up on the South Side. He's still the mayor, and bringing jobs to a town always looks good for politicians—even ones who aren't running for re-election."

I thinned my lips. My uncle would never do something good for the town just because it would help the people. If there wasn't money or power or both in it for him, he'd want no part of it.

Even becoming mayor years ago was about power and control for him.

There was more to it, and I planned to find out what it was. And, even if none of it made sense, I had a feeling it was connected to my uncle's sudden desire to be charitable by taking in Violet, Ava, and myself.

"Whatever you say. But if you hear anything suspicious, would you consider letting me know? I promise to take care of you. To make sure nothing happens to you."

He gave a half smile and nodded. "I'll try, but I can't promise, Knight."

I slapped him on the back and nodded. It was the best I could get from him, so I'd take it.

Walking him out, I noticed a car in the driveway next to his. Standing in the doorway, I watched as two girls stepped out of the black car.

Arabella and Violet.

My eyes slid down Violet's body. She was still wearing the school uniform from this morning. I stared at her plump lips as they frowned. She wasn't happy, and all I could think about was kissing her.

I hadn't expected Violet to come back so soon.

"What are you doing here?" Violet asked, pulling her backpack onto her shoulder. She had the same look on her face she had when she discovered me in art class the first day of school.

"I live here. And so do—"

"Not anymore." She held up her hand, effectively cutting me off. "I'm staying with Arabella. For. My. Safety."

"No." I wasn't about to take that shit. "I can't help you if you're at her house."

Arabella glared at me but stayed by her car as Violet pushed past me, stepping into the house. "I'm just here to collect my things. I texted my aunt. She knows not to come back here."

And then she turned to face me before

heading up the large curved dark wood staircase. With her brow raised, she uttered the words I feared she'd never utter, "Murderer."

I swallowed and shook my head. "It's not like that . . .. Violet." She dashed off up the stairs, and I wasn't far behind.

"Violet," I called out, but she ignored me.

Once she made it to her bedroom, she slammed the door. I tried to twist the knob, but she had locked it.

I knew banging on the door and demanding for her to let me in would be futile, so I used a different tactic.

Racing back to my room, I pulled on the bookcase that was the secret passage behind the walls. It didn't take me long to get up into the attic. I guess she had the same idea because I found her hiding up here.

"How did you get . . .? You know what? Don't answer that. I'm sure there are lots of ways to get up here that I don't know about."

She had taken off her school jacket and shoes. Violet stood there in a white blouse, short skirt, and cream-colored knee socks with her backpack at her feet. I had seen the uniform on countless girls, but the way Violet wore it caused my cock to stiffen.

I wanted her to stay and let me peel those clothes off her.

"Why did you call me a murderer?"

I had to focus on what had happened today, the news I got this morning, and what I had to do to protect her.

"Isn't that what you are? You murdered John Lenker and pinned it on me? I bet when we found the hole in the school basement, you figured you had a great hiding place for the body, and lucky for you, my prints were everywhere down there." She took a step forward and pushed her finger into my chest. "Well, guess what? Your prints are down there too."

She was right.

"I didn't kill that motherfucker. Sure, I wanted to beat the shit out of him after what he did to you with my uncle and that other guy, but I wouldn't actually kill him."

"Then why did you write those notes to me at school? The one in my locker and that one I got this morning."

My head went back in surprise. "What notes?"

She bent over, and I stared at her ass, her skirt inching up to reveal a slip of white cotton panties. I licked my lips, imagining nibbling on her flesh. It had been too long since I slipped my cock into her soaking wet pussy.

Her head angled to the side, and she

glanced up at me. "Get a good long look because that's all you're ever going to get."

She stood and shoved two pieces of paper in front of me.

After plucking them from her fingers, I read each, and my jaw tightened.

THREE

Violet

"**WHY DIDN'T YOU SHOW** these to me?" Knight said, throwing his arms up.

"Because you wrote them, that's why. Did you expect me to say thank you for the creepy love notes?"

He groaned, but I didn't care.

"No, I did not write them. If I'm going to threaten someone, I wouldn't be so cowardly as to leave notes. I'd do it to their face."

Knight wasn't a coward.

"I can see that." I shook my head. "But that still doesn't explain why you said *bye-bye* when I was being led to the police car earlier today. Look at the end of that note, which I found today in my locker."

His eyes skimmed the note again. I didn't need to look at it; the message was seared into my brain.

You tried to run, but I can hide. With you tucked neatly inside, all I have to do is lie. Say bye-bye.

Knight shrugged. "I was just trying to be indifferent. I've said bye-bye to Seraphina lots of times when she was being a bitch."

Suddenly, he didn't care?

"Being indifferent? You didn't care I was being hauled away for murder?"

His nostrils flared. "That's not what I meant. Damn it, I'm trying to tell you I had to pretend not to care because of who might be listening."

I shoved my hand on my hip. "And who would that be?"

"Someone working for my uncle. He's back in town. With his friend dead, he would pay attention to what was happening. I know some cops are on his payroll. If he thinks I don't care that you were arrested, he's less likely to do anything. To me or to you."

I sucked on my bottom lip as I pondered what he told me.

"If you didn't leave the notes or have me arrested . . . then who did?"

He took a step forward. Reaching up,

Knight slid his hand around the back of my neck. Shivers ran down my spine.

"I would never hurt you or let anyone hurt you. I'll find out who's behind this."

I hated that my body ached for his touch.

He pulled me close and leaned down, kissing my head. I felt him inhale. I shivered as he fisted his fingers in my hair.

"I need to taste you," Knight whispered.

He was warm, and, damn it, his embrace felt wonderful. Knight was a comforting cocoon in a fucked-up world.

That was how my heart felt, though my brain did not.

Warning bells were going off in my head, telling me to step away. But I couldn't.

He gripped my hair and pulled it back. Hundreds of pricks of pain burst over my scalp, and I moaned.

My mouth widened as I stared at his lips. They were wet, waiting for me to invite him to have a taste.

"Fuck, Violet. You're beautiful." His gaze skirted around my face.

For such an evil bastard, he could be lovely. I almost wanted him to be nasty. I wouldn't fall for him if he kept calling me trash. The edge I walked between sweet Knight and the devil was razor-thin. I felt each cut as I moved closer to him.

"Then kiss me," I said before lifting on my toes and licking his lip.

His mouth crashed on mine. I reached up and clung to his shirt.

When he walked out of his house earlier as Arabella drove up, I wondered how I would hold my ground against him. His sharp gray eyes sliced through me, and I almost walked straight into his arms instead of past him.

Then I remembered where I had been for the past several hours.

It was his touch that I couldn't resist. Knight saw straight into my soul. He was the puppet master, and I was his little broken doll.

He ground his hard cock into me. He might have been wearing jeans, but I remembered what was underneath.

I lifted my head and gasped, "Wait."

"Violet." The low rumble of the word radiated over my chest. My nipples hardened.

"I'm serious." I stepped back and caught my breath.

He stood there, hair mussed and lips swollen, and I wondered why I stopped in the first place.

"Is it because Arabella's outside? I can ask her to go away. Tell her you don't need to stay at her house anymore."

And there it was. That nagging uncertainty. Ever since I had known Knight, I felt it in the middle of my chest.

I shook my head. "No, I'm still staying with her."

He grew quiet, but the tick of his jaw told me exactly how he felt about me leaving.

He glared at me as he took a step back. "But I can't protect you if you leave."

While I was in lock up, I thought about him and all that had happened since coming to Green Hills Academy. I remembered my mom warning me, "*People with money only care about you if you can make them more money. If you can't, then you're nothing to them.*"

Knight had money. If I wasn't nothing to him, then that meant he was using me. But for what exactly?

"Why do you care so much about what happens to me?" I narrowed my eyes, ready for the truth.

He ran his fingers through his thick, dark hair. "Because you're different."

"You've said that before. I need more. Why do you hate your uncle so much? Is it because he stuck you in a mental hospital for a while?"

He took a step toward me until his body was flush with mine. I wanted to back up, but the room was too dark to see where I was going.

His chest rose and fell as his gaze bore into me. "You don't know what happened. You weren't there."

"No, I don't," I spit back, refusing to be intimidated. "And you won't tell me. You know why I hate your uncle, but I don't know why you do. I don't really know anything about you, Knight."

He took a breath and turned away from me. It felt cold in here without his touch. The one beam of light slashed across his face, and his eyes seemed hollow with the contrast.

"I haven't told anyone this, not even Briggs and Caleb. I explained some things to them, but not about what I believe really happened to my parents."

I remember that one reporter mentioned it when I first came to the mayor's home during that crazy press conference in the pool house.

"It was an accident. A plane crash. I heard from—"

"It wasn't an accident." He shook his head slowly.

"What?"

Knight turned to face me. Maybe it was the light, but he seemed tired.

"The plane . . . It was Jack Franklin's

plane. He owned Franklin First. If you think I have money, it's nothing compared to Jack's fortune."

"I heard of Franklin First. Isn't it a pharmaceutical company?"

He chuckled. "That and many other businesses. There's a media subsidiary, and a grocery store chain, property development company—both residential and commercial—along with a few smaller companies."

"Wow. That's a wide variety."

"My parents invested in Franklin First Laboratories because my dad was a scientist and believed in what Jack was doing."

"What was he doing?"

Knight rubbed his chin. "He was finding a cure for cancer. I don't know if it was for a specific cancer or if it even worked, but that's what my dad told me."

"That's amazing. So, what happened?"

"The crash," he said with a sigh. "The board took over, and the cancer drug, well . . . I have no idea what happened to it."

I took a step forward and placed my hand on his arm. He reached over, brushing his thumb across my fingers before bringing them to his mouth to kiss.

"I know you're wondering what this has to do with me hating my uncle or the crash not being an accident. And the truth is, I don't know."

"But—"

"I know what I said . . . that the plane crash wasn't an accident. It's what I learned about my uncle once I came here. There was something he said to Kiki a week after Ava and I moved in. I overheard him tell her that the plan was working. And now that they had the kids, they could take control."

"What?" My eyes widened. If what Knight said was true, it sounded like his uncle had something to do with it.

"I was so angry after I heard him, I devised a plan to hurt him. Nothing serious . . . just make him sick. I slipped something in his food."

"Knight," I gasped.

"I was sixteen; it wasn't like I was thinking straight. Someone told him I tried to poison him. He thought I was trying to kill him, and he had me committed." He rubbed his brow. "But that backfired. It only made me more determined to find out the truth. What was his plan, and why did he need us to do it?"

"And . . .?"

"I still don't know. But it involves you, too. I don't understand how, but it has something to do with your mother."

Memories of my mom the night before she died came flooding back. It was strange she kept telling me she loved me. I thought it was nerves because she was about to get her one-year chip for being sober.

But what if it had to do with more than just that? What if it had to do with what Knight was telling me?

I wanted to discover the truth as much as Knight, but I didn't want to be used to get it.

"Is that why you bailed me out? To keep me at your side. Because I might come in handy getting information from your uncle? I'm not a pawn in your sick family feud."

"It's more than that, Violet." He kissed my hand once more before releasing it. "At first, yes, I wanted you to live in the house so I could keep an eye on you. Find out anything on my uncle. But the last several weeks have been so much more."

I stepped back, glancing down so I wouldn't trip over anything. "No."

He tilted his head. "Excuse me?"

"No, I don't believe you. I may not have known you long, but where I come from, everyone has an angle. And I know yours."

His eyes narrowed. "And what's my . . . angle?"

"Power. Control. Just like your uncle." I watched his jaw tick, but I wasn't about to stop. "You say you're nothing like him, yet here you are . . . digging up dirt on him and blaming him for the problems in your life."

"But he tried to rape y—"

"I know what he did to me. But I'm not here using people. Manipulating everyone to bring him down. That's you. Just like he has done."

I watched the wrinkle in his forehead smooth as my words took hold.

"I like you, Knight. I know I shouldn't, but I do. And it's because I like you that I have to leave and live with Arabella."

I turned and found the ladder that led out of the attic.

"Violet, I need to protect you."

I sighed. "And I need to tell the truth. Lies have destroyed so much of my life. I watched it destroy my mother. And if I stay here, I know at some point you'll get me to lie. And that's not me."

I made my way down the stairs and into my bedroom to pack. It surprised me that he left me alone.

And when I came back out to the driveway, throwing my suitcase into Arabella's trunk, I saw him stare down from one window. I waved, but he turned and left.

FOUR

Violet

THE WATER DROPLETS SLID down the window. I thought of when I was little and was stuck inside on a rainy day. How I'd bet myself which droplet would win.

Now the bet was between my heart and

Knight. When I woke up this morning, after walking away from him yesterday, it felt like he was winning.

"We're here. Get ready for some retail therapy," Arabella said as she popped open her car door.

Opening the passenger door, I stepped out into the dark garage. The place was filled with so many pricey cars that they could cover the GDP of a small country.

"I have seen this mall before, but I've never been inside it."

"My mom used to take me here all the time when I was little. Get me cute things and dress me up like a doll." Her grin faltered as we moved closer to the large glass entrance surrounded by an even bigger marble frame.

"I take it she doesn't live around here anymore."

I hadn't asked about her mom before.

She told me on the first day of school that her mom left when she was five and that she rarely saw her. It sounded like a touchy subject, so I never brought it up.

The doors opened thanks to the help of two men dressed in tuxedos. My gaze slid to one who stared straight ahead like a zombie butler.

“No. Last I heard, she was in Paris. Or maybe it was London. Who cares?” She took a breath and plastered on a smile. “We’re here to cheer you up. Where do you want to go first? Clothes or food or the spa?”

I glanced down at my arm. “Definitely not the spa. No touching my body.”

“Okay, then food. If you’re hungry, they have an amazing sushi place—”

“Not really hungry. How about clothes?”

I gave a half smile, wondering how I

was going to try on anything over my arm brace. I loved Arabella, and it was nice that she wanted to cheer me up, but I was more of a homebody. Hanging out at the mall wasn't my thing.

"Great, we can go to Chella's. They'll serve us champagne." She elbowed me.

My mind kept drifting back to Knight. The closer I got to him, the more confused I became. He put up the money to bail me out and said he didn't write those notes, but he was related to the mayor.

He had been in a mental hospital. Could I believe anything that came out of his mouth?

"Earth to Violet." Arabella snapped her fingers.

"Sorry." I shook my head with a laugh. "I'm still a little skittish about being arrested. Should I even show my face out in public right now?"

She stopped me right before we

entered Chella's Boutique. The place looked stark, with only a few dozen pieces of clothing hung along the wall. Instead of racks in the middle of the shop, there were three green velvet couches surrounding a large marble coffee table.

A woman in a pale blue blouse and brown plaid skirt stood by the wall pretending to adjust a coat hanging near her, but I noticed her gaze drift toward us.

"You didn't kill him," she said with a snort. "It's laughable that the police are even considering it. You weigh like ninety-eight pounds soaking wet, and he was a middle-aged guy."

I remembered John Lenker being tall with a not-so-lean middle. He had to weigh at least two hundred pounds, if not more.

I rolled my eyes. "I weigh over ninety-eight pounds."

She waved her hand. “Whatever. The point is, how would you have been able to drag a large, heavy body all the way down into that basement alone? Impossible.”

It was crazy, but I wasn’t wealthy with lots of expensive lawyers at my disposal. The best I could hope for was that the public defender wasn’t a complete moron.

“I guess . . .” I mumbled.

She placed her hand on my good arm. “Violet. You have people who care about you. Don’t worry. We will take care of you. And Knight, as much of a dickhole as he is normally, seems to like you. If you have him on your side, then I wouldn’t be surprised if the police drop the charges.”

I was about to ask her more about Knight. How could an eighteen-year-old high schooler have so much power?

But a nasally, whiny voice that reminded me of nails on a chalkboard cut me off.

"If it isn't the *murderer.* Aren't you supposed to be in jail?" Seraphina came up to me and poked my bad shoulder.

I sucked in a breath through my teeth.

Fucking bitch.

"Aren't you supposed to go for silicone refills? They look a little . . . deflated." I scrunched my nose and pointed at her tits with a mock pout.

Her face turned red, and I thought for sure she'd scream so loud it'd shatter all the mirrors in the boutique.

But an older woman with gorgeous chestnut brown hair came up behind Seraphina and placed a hand on her shoulder. She looked like an older version of Seraphina, but with the darker hair and not so much plastic.

"Honey, you know what the doctor said about your temper. Take deep breaths," she told Seraphina.

And like an angel sent from bitch-reform-school heaven, Seraphina did as she was told.

She exhaled. "Sorry, Mommy. It's just . . . this is the girl who killed Shawna's dad. I saw the police arrest her."

Mrs. Hillingham's eyes widened for only a second before they calmly slid to me. "Oh, Seraphina, you must be joking. She couldn't possibly have done that. Look at her. She'd probably topple over if she tried to lift my Hermes bag."

The woman shook her head, and as Seraphina opened her mouth, her mom made a tutting sound. Faster than you could say *Ankle Bitch*, Seraphina nodded and replied, "Yes, Mommy."

I liked her. Anyone who could put Seraphina in her place with just a sound was a queen in my book.

All hail, Mrs. Hillingham.

She stretched out her hand. "I don't believe we have met before. I'm Crystal Hillingham."

I hesitated and glanced over at Arabella. Was this a trap? If I touched her, would Seraphina and her mom take me down, all a prank to dupe the girl who didn't belong?

Arabella nudged me, urging me on.

My hand trembled as I took her hand to shake. It was what I expected, cold and limp.

My mother had lots of theories about the wealthy, and their handshakes were one of them. She said that wealthy, powerful men had some sort of macho thing going on where they had to prove they were superior with intense handshakes.

Whereas wealthy women were the

opposite. It was almost bad manners to greet someone with a firm shake—the weaker the hand, the more money they had.

I tried not to crush her hand as I lifted it up and down gently.

"My, but you are pretty," Crystal cooed with a grin.

"Thank you."

"And your friend?" She waved at Arabella.

"Oh, sorry, right. This is Arabella."

Arabella introduced herself, and Seraphina pointed out that her dad was the principal.

"Yes, Mr. Lyndon. It's been a while since we spoke. I hope he is well."

Arabella nodded, and I wondered how long we had to stand here before we could escape the awkwardness of the situation. Yes, I now worshiped Crystal for her power over her daughter, but she was a mom. And being a teenager, I didn't really hang out with moms.

"Were you two ladies about to buy something at Chella's?"

"I don't know about buy. Just look around," I mentioned.

There was no way I could afford anything here or any store in the mall itself. I might have been able to afford an overpriced churro at the food court, if they had a food court. They probably had private chefs stationed in well-hidden alcoves, because heaven forbid the wealthy were spotted doing something so pedestrian as eat food.

"Nonsense." She shuffled us inside, placing her hand on my back. "What is the point of coming all this way without going home with something? And by the looks of your arm, you deserve to indulge, Violet."

The sales assistant I noticed earlier appeared with a red smile and sparkling blue eyes pointed directly at Crystal.

"Mrs. Hillingham. It's so wonderful to see you again. And you brought your daughter and her friends. How lovely." I got an intense whiff of her perfume, and it must have been that new one called *eau de ass-kiss.*

I watched as the older Hillingham directed the associate around the store like it was her home and she was the maid.

It wasn't long before we were seated on the couches sipping champagne—just as Arabella had said—and there were actual models walking around in clothes we picked out to see how they looked.

None of us tried on a single thing. And the best part was Seraphina did her best to glare at me, but her mom caught her every time.

"Mommy, I'm supposed to go to Lilla's house for lunch."

Crystal's perfectly sculpted brow rose. "It's so rare we get to spend time together. And your eighteenth birthday is only weeks away. I just wanted to spend some mother-daughter time together before you're not my little girl anymore."

Seraphina's lips thinned as she stood from the couch. "Mom, we've had my entire life for that. It's just a lunch."

"What do you think, Violet? Don't you like spending time with your mom?" Crystal asked in a tone that was relaxed.

Perhaps it was the question that threw me off, but I swore her expression didn't match her tone. Sure, she was smiling, but it felt forced.

I rubbed my brow. "My mom is dead," I said in a whisper.

"Oh, dear." Crystal brought her hand

to her mouth. “I am so sorry. I had no idea.”

“Yes, you did, Mommy. This is the girl Knight found at Happy Pond. Remember?” Seraphina waved at me like I was one skirt she decided not to buy.

“Right.” Crystal appeared pained. “I’m sorry. My memory isn’t what it used to be. Stress, I suppose.”

She turned toward me and placed her hand on mine. “I’m sorry if my question brought up a terrible memory.”

I felt the tears rising. With a hitched breath, I pushed the heartache back. “It’s alright. You didn’t know.”

The corner of her mouth ticked up right before she announced, “Since my daughter wants to leave us, why don’t I treat both of you to lunch?”

My brows lifted, and I glanced over at Arabella. She shrugged and said, “Why not?"

If Arabella was fine with eating a meal with Seraphina's mom, then I guess I was too.

As we made our way out of the boutique with bags of clothes both Arabella and Crystal bought me, I leaned over and whispered to Arabella, "Didn't you used to be friends with Seraphina?"

"Yes. But I never actually met her parents before. Only Knight was allowed inside Seraphina's house. Apparently, she had an elderly grandmother who couldn't handle loud noises. And kids make noise."

That made sense. But what made little sense was how polar opposite Crystal Hillingham was from her daughter. Perhaps with Crystal on my side, Seraphina would ease off me.

FIVE

Violet

I STOOD THERE STARING at the large wooden double doors. The carving on the front was an intricate crest. There was no doubt the door was old, perhaps original to the building, brought over from Europe. But it was the darkness it represented that caused me to hesitate.

"I promise, it won't bite. The most you'll get is a splinter," Arabella said with a chuckle as she stepped beside me.

"A week ago, I walked through the Green Hills Academy door and was arrested twenty minutes later. It's not like the weeks leading up to the arrest were peaches and cream."

"Mmm. Peaches. I could really go for a peach. Too bad it's October."

I rolled my eyes. "I'm serious. Don't make fun of my anxiety."

She gasped, clutching her chest. "Me too. There isn't much in life better than a good peach."

"Now I know what to get you for your birthday. Speaking of which, when is your birthday?"

"In a month. I'm a Scorpio baby. Roar." She pretended to claw the air with her fingers.

"A scorpion doesn't roar . . . they sting."

"Tell that to the baseball team's backs." She wiggled her eyebrows.

"Oh my god—"

"Hey, Violet." Seraphina waved at me as she strolled past.

Both my mouth and Arabella's mouth fell open.

"Did you just say hi to me?" I pointed at myself.

Based on the size of her bitch squad's eyes, they couldn't believe it either.

"Yes. I just loved our outing at the mall last week. We have to do it again."

I had no idea what was going on. Was she trying to lure me into some false sense of security before she pounced? That had to be it.

"I can't really—"

"Seraphina, she's a murderer. She

killed my dad," Shawna said as she glared in my direction.

I was about to explain that I had no part in his death—though I dreamed of it many times—but Seraphina beat me to it.

"Shut up, Shawna." Seraphina turned her cold blue gaze on her friend. "They dropped those charges. Remember?"

They did?

"I didn't hear about that," I said, wondering how Seraphina knew that, yet me, the supposed murderer, did not.

"Yes, please. It was all so stupid. They had the wrong prints or something. I don't know about that stuff. My mom contacted the sheriff and got the *right* answers." She winked at me.

"Your mom had the charges dropped?" Arabella, who looked as dumbfounded as I felt, asked.

"Not really. The charges were about to

be dropped when recent evidence appeared. And, really, Violet is too small to do what was done to that body."

"Seraphina," Shawna said as her voice cracked.

"Look, Shawna, I am sorry your dad died. Okay? But this depressing act you're putting on is pathetic. Get over it, girl. He's dead. Move on." Seraphina pushed her hands on her hips and glared at Shawna.

"Seraphina, that's not nice to say—" I tried to stick up for the girl, but she wanted none of it.

"Shut up, you bitch!" Shawna screamed as tears flowed down her cheeks. "All you are is trailer trash. Everything was fine before your skanky ass showed up. You have everyone fooled, but not me."

Shawna stomped her feet and ran to the door of the school. She threw open the door before the attendant could get to it and disappeared inside.

"She must have woken up on the bitch side of the bed this morning," Seraphina commented as her one remaining bitch squad friend, Harlow, awkwardly giggled.

"I have to get inside so—" I wanted out of the crazy opposite-day moment I had encountered.

"Violet, I'm classy enough to admit I haven't been the nicest person to you since you got here six weeks ago. But that's about to change . . .. We need each other. Us girls. There are guys here," she glanced around the front of the school before leaning toward me, "who would love to pit us against each other. Only to break us down. One guy in particular. And I was silly enough to fall for it. But not anymore."

"But you locked me on a bus, and I nearly died because of it."

Her cheeks flushed as she held up her hands. "I had no idea the brakes were defective on that bus. It was a little prank. That door should have easily opened. Trust me, my dad is having all our busses inspected so nothing like that happens again."

I narrowed my eyes. It was like her words were perfectly crafted, but I heard the twinge of insincerity in her tone.

Despite that, I did what I had to do to get away from her.

"Apology accepted," I said and felt Arabella's elbow in my side.

"Great." Her eyes slid down my body, and I couldn't help but notice a faint sneer cross her lips. "You really need a tailor. But we can discuss that at lunch. Bye." She waved at me and left, with Harlow eagerly on her tail.

"That was so fucking weird," Arabella

murmured.

"Did I wake up in an alternate universe where Seraphina likes me?"

"I don't know. I guess if her mom likes you, that means she has to like you. Or maybe it has something to do with the bus accident. She doesn't want to be sued. And this might be a good thing."

I jerked my head at her. "A good thing? Anything involving Seraphina can't be a good thing."

"You know the old saying: keep your friends close and your enemies closer. You might find out something if you let her '*like*' you," she air-quoted.

"I guess." I was hesitant to like Seraphina back. "Maybe that's why her mom was so nice. Once she realized who I was last Thursday at the mall, she made nice so I wouldn't sue her family's company. I can't believe I didn't think of that myself."

"That's why I'm here. To help put the complicated pieces of your life together for you."

"Whatever would I do without you, Arabella?"

She shook her head and giggled. "You'd still be roaming the halls looking for your locker." She placed her hand on my back, and we moved to the front door.

Once we were inside, I waved goodbye to Arabella as she made her morning trip to her father's office, and I took the stairs to my locker.

When I turned the corner, there were a few students at their lockers, but one didn't belong. And he was standing right in front of my locker.

Knight.

He leaned against it, his dark hair tousled and gray eyes targeting me. My heart shifted, making room for the fire he ignited.

Slowing my steps to my locker, I wasn't in any hurry to discover why Knight waited for me. I'd kept my distance for almost a week, and I wasn't about to stop doing that just because we were in the same building.

"I'm not going anywhere," he said, jerking his chin toward me.

"But I am." I stood in front of him and waved toward the locker door, ignoring the spicy scent that wafted from his skin. "Therefore, I need my stuff."

He took a step back, and I unlocked the door to my locker and opened it, letting out a breath as it blocked my view of him. His fingers slid over mine as I clutched the door. My mind raced with dirty thoughts of all the times he used those fingers on me.

Knight pulled the door back flat against the locker next to mine. "You need to come home."

My eyes slid to him. "I need to get to class."

He smiled in that arrogant way that both irritated me and made my panties all wet.

"It's not about me."

Groaning, I reached in and grabbed my things before shoving the locker closed. "It's always about you, Knight. Before I stepped foot into the school, I heard about you. How you're the king of the school. You used me for your own benefit to get to your uncle."

"That's not entirely true."

I titled my head and shifted my backpack on my shoulder. "Isn't it? Because I've had some time to think about the past six weeks, and everything I went through seemed to involve you. Even the day I was stuck on the bus at Winter Rivers University. Seraphina had told me you went to visit her the night before . . . made it seem like you two were together again. Is that true?"

What Seraphina told me this morning was starting to get to me. What if she was right? What if he had played both of us?

His jaw tightened. "I went to visit her that night."

It felt as if my heart fell out of my chest and shattered on the floor. I lifted my chin, refusing to gift him with my pain.

"I guess I was just another fuck then, huh?" I felt my voice wobble, so I pushed past him.

"Violet, I needed . . ."

He drifted away as I quickened my pace and weaved in between other students. I was thankful that today we didn't have art class.

Seraphina might have been a shallow bitch, but Knight could easily hurt her too. Perhaps she wasn't my enemy after all—and it was the devil all along.

SIX

Violet

"ANOTHER RALLY? REALLY?" I groaned as I scooted next to Arabella.

"Now you see why I hate them so much," she said, nudging me.

"Considering the last one showed a film of me undressing, I have every reason to hate them too." My fingers slipped over the locket that hung from my neck.

She frowned. "Oh yeah, I almost forgot. Shit. So much has happened to you since. You're like the bad-luck queen. No offense."

"None taken."

I shook the terrible memories of that rally out of my head, instead replacing them with what Knight did to my body in the locker room after. Heat crawled up my neck, and I glanced around, hoping no one noticed my obvious blush.

I hadn't seen Knight since he stalked me at my locker earlier this morning. Even at lunch, he was nowhere to be found. Seraphina, on the other hand, was suddenly my new best friend. She came over to our table during lunch, dragging Harlow with her.

Harlow didn't approve of me

becoming her friend's latest bestie, but she went along with Seraphina like a loyal puppy slurping up treats.

And don't get me wrong . . . I didn't approve either. But the more Seraphina talked at lunch, the more I realized how pathetic she sounded. It was obvious affection was considered a weakness in her home.

"Oh, no," Arabella said with a groan.

"What—" I glanced up to discover Seraphina waving at us.

Her wide smile, with teeth that gleamed like a lighthouse in the fog, grew the moment she spotted me.

"She's psycho. I mean, I said she was a crazy bitch before, but I meant that more in a I-hate-you-crazy-bitch sort of way. Now I seriously think she needs medical help." I turned to face Arabella, hoping that somehow once Seraphina saw the back of my head, she'd lose interest.

It was a long shot, but I was desperate.

"Oh. My. God. Bitch, I've been looking everywhere for you," Seraphina said with too much excitement.

My shoulders slumped, and I glanced up at her. "Been here the whole time." My lips tightened, and I mumbled, "I'm kind of wishing it was my body found in that hole right about now."

Arabella heard me and giggled.

"What?" Seraphina tilted her head.

I had the feeling if there wasn't so much Botox in her forehead, her brow would be wrinkled right now.

I waved my hand at her. "Nothing."

Glancing around the stadium seats in the gym, I noticed some students were staring at us. They were just as confused as I was that Seraphina had sat next to me.

"Oh, look, the rally's starting." I

pointed to the gym floor, hoping it would distract Seraphina.

I noticed Knight wasn't here. Again. He wasn't at the last rally either.

Seraphina leaned over and whispered, "He never comes."

Okay . . . that was eerie.

"Who?" I eyed her with suspicion. Could she read my mind?

"Knight."

My mouth hung open. How did she know that was what I was thinking?

"I saw you looking around for someone." She shrugged. "I assumed it was Knight. But don't worry, he won't show up. For the past two years, since his parents died, he's skipped them. The teachers look past it because, you know . . ." she trailed off and swirled her finger by her head, showing that he was crazy.

I sat up straight. What she said

bothered me, though it shouldn't have. From what I knew about the guy, it was not that much of a surprise that he had some issues.

But all the same, I felt like defending him. Maybe it was because I hated Seraphina so much.

The principal walked out and addressed the students. He told us the assembly was a little different this time because of recent discoveries at the school.

"My dad means the body," Arabella said.

"Fuck. Can't we please move on?" Seraphina rolled her eyes.

There was some murmuring from the surrounding kids while some eyes turned to me. I knew why. They had arrested me. It didn't matter that they had cleared me; in a few of these kids' eyes, I was always going to be guilty.

"What is everyone staring at?" Seraphina's voice rose. "She didn't do it, you idiots."

I blinked. Seraphina was defending me to the students.

And just like that, everyone turned back to face the front. I smirked. Maybe it wasn't so bad to have Seraphina on my side.

Arabella leaned over and whispered, "Milk this for all it's worth."

I nodded. I knew what she meant. Seraphina would never be someone I would be close to, but it didn't mean I couldn't use her to help me. It may not be the best way to treat a person, but it wasn't like she had done much over the past six weeks to deserve better.

As I stared at Seraphina, I didn't notice the man who walked out to the center of the gym and stood in front of the microphone. Not until the students erupted in applause.

I felt all the blood drain from my face as my gaze fell upon my living, breathing nightmare.

The mayor.

“Thank you, everyone. Please.” He gave that megawatt smile that had me fooled once and waved for everyone to stop clapping.

I could barely hear the students as the beating of my heart grew louder in my ears. Arabella’s hand gripped mine. She frowned, and I was so struck with fear, I couldn’t move.

The mayor studied the crowd, but he had yet to spot me. I took solace in that. Maybe his speech would be short, and then he’d leave, never noticing me.

“It’s great to be back at my old alma mater. Some of the best times of my life were spent right here, roaming these halls." He winked.

The students chuckled as I shivered. I bet he was a rapist then too. That was probably what he was referring to—trapping girls wherever he could.

My stomach flipped, and I covered my mouth. *Don't puke, Violet. Keep it together.*

"But that's not why I came here today. It's about a good friend of mine, John Lenker. He was the one found in the basement."

There was a flutter of gasps. I thought back to how good of a friend he was to the mayor. They shared everything, including me.

"And I know if it were your friend down there, you'd do everything in your power to find that terrible murderer too. So, let me make this crystal clear. That's exactly what I plan to do. I will devote the rest of my time as mayor to capturing John Lenker's murderer. And when I make promises, I always keep them." His biting gray eyes locked onto me.

I whimpered as I still felt his fingers dig into my thighs.

He spoke some more, moving his gaze from me to the crowd, but I didn't hear a thing. The mayor was going to make sure I took the fall for John's murder, no matter what. He must have been the person who called in the tip to the police that got me arrested.

I wanted out of the gym, to run away. Not to hide in the locker room like last time or even to stay the rest of the day at Arabella's.

I meant disappear. I needed to hop a train or hitch a ride or something that took me far away from his world.

And it was at that moment I felt

something I was sure was the grip of death coming to take me. Fingers wrapped around my ankle and pulled.

I yelped.

The mayor stopped talking, and the entire school turned to look at me.

Did the mayor do that on purpose? Did he pay someone to try to pull me under the bleachers? The way he was watching me with confusion written all over his face, I suspected not.

“It’s almost over,” Arabella whispered to me.

I wasn’t screaming for that reason, but I wasn’t about to tell her that.

Seraphina frowned and turned her back to me. No one knew why I had screamed, and I was almost too scared to look at what was under the benches.

Maybe it was a thug with a baseball bat whom the mayor had hired, or worse.

I sucked up a breath and bent down, acting as if I were searching inside my backpack. It was dark under the bleachers, and I had to squint to see. I moved closer to the darkness, and that was when I saw his gray eyes.

He slid his finger up to his lips to indicate for me to be quiet.

It was Knight.

Did that make it better? No. But of the two evils, one speaking and the other hiding, Knight was the lesser of the two.

I tapped Arabella on her knee and pointed down. She nodded.

She assumed I was going to hide from the mayor, which I was, but she didn't know Knight was waiting for me.

I glanced around and saw that everyone was watching the mayor, even Seraphina. That was when I made my move and slid through the bleacher seats.

It was tight and with my hurt arm, it wasn't easy, but I felt Knight's hand on my legs as I worked my way through.

I had been high up, so it was a jump to the ground. He held on tight, and a bolt of awareness shot through me. Even now, with the mayor so close, Knight's touch had the power to melt the chaos away.

My feet hit the gym floor with a thud. Rubbing my shoulder, I turned, the soles of my shoes squeaking as I did. And as my gaze fell on the boy who pulled me into this world when he found me on the boat at Happy Pond, I sucked in a breath through my teeth.

He was gorgeous, and I hated him for that. From his dark, fuck-me hair to his sharp cheekbones, Knight was the kind of guy who could get anything from anyone if he gave them a smile. But he rarely did that.

And the only way he got anything from me was if he gave me orgasms. That thought saddened me. Was I really so pathetic?

"What are you doing here?" I hissed as I tried to look at everything except Knight.

"I heard he would be here, and I wasn't about to let him see me." Knight pointed in between the bleacher bench seats.

"It's not like you come to these rallies, anyway. But why me?" I placed my hand on my chest, trying to hide my rapid breathing.

He was only inches from me. The air I breathed smelled of sweat, floor cleaner, and Knight. And as the kids above me clapped and hollered, my clit throbbed with want to be touched by the boy in front of me.

And I knew he wasn't a good guy. He would probably use my body and walk away once he got what he wanted from me. But as I stood there watching him lean against one of the metal poles holding the seats up, I wanted his hands on me, taking anything he wanted.

"Because you never let me explain what happened with Seraphina. Why I went over to her house."

The only reason I agreed to hear him out was because I needed to stay hidden.

"Fine. So tell me."

He ran his fingers through his hair, making it look even sexier, as if that were possible.

"I didn't sleep with her. I haven't fucked Seraphina since spring."

I held up my hands. "Not relevant. Don't need to hear the last time you banged that bouncing bag of Botox."

He smirked and nodded. "Okay. I went over there to get my phone back. She hadn't put everything back in my locker. She did it on purpose to get me to talk to her. It worked. But she didn't realize I would take the phone and leave, and not stick around for her slut show."

What she said earlier about him using both of us was bothering me.

"Why do you hate her so much? Did she cheat on you or something?"

"I see you've gotten on her good side. Was that to piss me off?"

The fact that he didn't answer the question didn't go unnoticed. If he wanted to play the dodge-question game, then I could play it too.

"Why don't you want me to be friends with her? She actually stood up for me in front of the entire school up there." I pointed to where I had been seated. "Seraphina may not be the nicest person, but perhaps that's because of how people have treated her."

I didn't know who was more surprised by what came out of my mouth—Knight or me.

He took a step closer, and I stepped back until another pole hit my spine.

His nostrils flared as he narrowed his eyes at me. "You're seriously defending her? And what about me? Getting you out of jail and making sure you didn't get raped . . . is that nothing to you?"

"No, it's not nothing. I'm not saying that. But you won't tell me anything."

"Fine, you want to know why I hate Seraphina? Because this past June, I found out it wasn't my uncle's idea to put me away. It was hers."

My eyes widened, and I was about to ask him how he found out, but I heard the kids above us get up. I looked up and realized the rally was over. I knew I should leave, should blend into the crowd so the mayor wouldn't notice me, but I had to learn more about what had happened to Knight.

When I gazed back to where Knight stood, he was nowhere to be found. I searched around, but he must have had the same idea of mixing in with the students.

I didn't trust Knight, but at least I was getting some answers about his life.

SEVEN

Knight

My eyes flicked to the large glass window that looked out onto the street. A few people walked by, but not the one I was waiting for. I took a breath and inhaled the rich scent of coffee.

Lifting my paper cup, I took a sip of

the hot, black liquid pick-me-up sweetened with four packets of raw sugar. I wondered if I should leave.

He was twenty minutes late, and I was skipping English class for our appointment.

I came straight here after the rally. I wanted to stay and talk more with Violet, but I couldn't. The meeting was too important.

A throat cleared. Turning my head, I saw a man covering his mouth to cough, seated at one of the many square pine tables in The Drip.

Turning back to face the window, I shook my head. It was time to leave. Right as I shifted and placed my hands on the table, I felt someone touch my shoulder.

"Sorry I'm late," Edwin said as he slid into the black metal seat across from me, and the tiny table wobbled. A drip of my coffee slipped through the tiny hole in the lid, sliding down the side.

"I have to get back. My teacher is pretty lenient, but the threat of exposing an online gambling habit will only get me so far."

"Right. Well, there isn't much that needs to be said." Edwin reached into his suit jacket pocket and plucked out a thick white envelope. "Here." His fingers pushed it toward me.

My eyes shifted around the room. No one was paying any attention to us. I opened the envelope and pulled out the papers. They were thick stock, cream-colored, and reminded of something I had seen before.

"Have you ever had to deliver something to Green Hills Academy before?"

Edwin nodded. "Of course. Many times. Why?"

"An envelope like this?"

He shrugged. "A few times."

"Did you know what was in the

envelope?"

"No. I figured if he was delivering something to a school, then it's not really of any interest to me."

I scratched my chin. I believed I knew who was sending Violet those notes.

"Who did you deliver them to?"

Edwin sat up. "Just to the front office, and then they contacted whoever it was for. And before you ask, I just told them it was from the mayor's office and didn't pay attention to who it was addressed to."

It could have been someone in the office or any student. At least I knew someone at Green Hills Academy was working with my uncle. But who?

I lowered my gaze to the pieces of paper in my hand. They were emails, and the final one looked like a contract.

"This is for a possible cancer drug called E-L100. From Franklin First Pharmaceuticals. It looks like my uncle invested in it, and they set it to enter phase one of the trials a few years ago. Why is this relevant to me?"

Edwin leaned over and pointed to the contract. I scanned it, and my eyes widened.

"But this says there were two other investors, and the drug failed the first phase. Why did they invest after it failed?"

Edwin nodded. "That's the same question I asked myself. And look at the amount they had invested. Why throw that much money at something that doesn't work?"

"Do you know who the other investors are?"

He sighed. "No. I looked, but I couldn't find anything."

"Knight. Knight King, is that you?" A female voice came from behind.

I quickly shuffled the papers back into the envelope and shoved it into my navy uniform jacket.

"Mrs. Hillingham." I plastered a smile

on my face as I gazed up at Seraphina's mom.

Her tailored brown plaid pencil skirt fit her well. I'd be lying if I said I hadn't imagined bending her over a few times and sinking my cock deep inside her. I bet she knew exactly how to work my cock.

But she was related to Seraphina, and if Seraphina was insane, then I bet she got it from her mom.

"Aren't you supposed to be in school?" Her red lips curled as she sashayed her way over to my table.

I stood and held up my hands. "You caught me. Playing hooky to go over some legal documents."

Her blue eyes sparkled with merriment as she let out a throaty laugh. "Just like your father, always work-minded. If he were still alive, I know he'd be proud of you." She reached over and squeezed my shoulder.

Would he? He was always by the book,

always explained the importance of following the rules. But in the past two years, I lost count of how many laws I broke to seek the truth.

I wondered sometimes if he would have done the same thing? Maybe not.

"Thank you." I nodded. "Mrs. Hillingham, this is Edwin—"

"Oh, we have met. Mr. Locklear, it's been a while. Nice to see you." She held out her hand, and Edwin stood, causing the chair to scrape loudly against the floor.

"Yes, it's been a while. A few years. At the Green Hills Pumpkin Luncheon you threw," Edwin said as he shook her hand.

She lowered her hand and winked. "It's the best time of the year. It's too bad he didn't make it last year. Please tell him he's invited to this year's luncheon. It's for a good cause. A new state-of-the-art drug rehabilitation facility. I know how important it is for him to give to the community."

"Yes, elicit is running rampant in South Green Hills," Edwin said.

I nodded. "Some friend of mine had some problems with it. A kid in school overdosed last year."

She frowned. "It's so scary. And I feel for those families. That's why I felt obligated to dedicate this year's luncheon to raising money for the best facility so we could help them."

"I assume your husband is donating too?" I asked.

Her nose flared, and she glanced away for a second before looking back with a wide smile. "You know Mr. Hillingham. Work, work, work, but he has promised money for the cause. I just wish he could be there too."

I remembered Seraphina's parents not having the best marriage. Not that I thought her husband cheated on her, but I had overheard some fights—usually about their business.

"I have to head back to school. It was nice to see you, Mrs. Hillingham." I turned to Edwin and nodded. "Thanks."

They waved me off, and I headed to my red Audi R8 parked along the street. Once I got to school, I parked the car myself. I didn't trust those parking attendants with my car.

Once I was inside the school, I saw the hallway was filled with students. Perfect timing, classes had just let out.

It was last period, and I had history. Making my way toward the history wing, I saw something that stopped me in my tracks.

Seraphina was strolling down the hallway, giggling with Violet at her side. She wasn't laughing at Violet, but with her. As if they were friends.

What. The. Hell?

I stayed back and watched. Right as they were about to turn the corner, Seraphina glanced over her shoulder and saw me. She winked, and then they turned, disappearing out of sight.

She was up to something. That bitch would never be friends with someone who couldn't help her. Unless Violet had a mysterious wealthy relative that only Seraphina knew about, I knew she was doing this to hurt me or to hurt Violet. Probably both.

Fuck.

Now I wasn't just worried about my uncle hurting Violet, but now I had to watch Seraphina too.

EIGHT

Violet

"YOU ALL HAVE A folded piece of paper in your hand. Do not open it until I tell you," our art teacher, Ms. Chiron, said as she waved her hands in the air.

I held my hand above my eyes to shield the sun. It was Wednesday, and we were outside for class. I sat under a tree near the tennis courts while enjoying the light breeze.

Ms. Chiron thought the October day was too beautiful to be spent indoors for class, and she was right. I filled my lungs with the scent of dying leaves and freshly cut grass.

The boys, Knight and his crew, sat nearby, huddled together like they were planning an escape. Only Knight glanced back at me every so often. He had been stalking me over the last two days since I found him at my locker on Monday.

Maybe they weren't planning to get away, but to grab me instead.

"Today is the perfect day to announce your autumn projects." There were loud groans from the scattered students around her.

Her hands waved in the air. "This year you will pair up with a partner. You two will have to work as a creative team to impress me with your art. Most artists work alone, and therefore, this will be a challenge. But in the real world, you will need to accept direction and limitations on what can be done. Whether it be a future boss or colleague or client. This project will help you learn how to deal with that."

I closed my eyes, and for once in my life, I prayed. *Don't let me be stuck with Knight or any of his crew.*

I glanced over once I opened them again and found Knight staring at me.

"Okay, students, open your paper. See who you will work with for the next month."

I took a breath and unfolded my piece of paper.

"Fuck," I mumbled to myself.

Knight King was there in black and white. No chance of me misreading or it being smudged and therefore a different name. His name had been typed.

I crumpled up the paper, and when I glanced up, a figure stood before me blocking out the sun.

"I guess we're partners," Knight said.

I fidgeted with my pencil as my heart slammed against my chest at the sight of him.

"Looks like it," I mumbled.

He crouched until his lips were inches from mine, and I couldn't help but stare at them. They curled, and all I wanted to do was kiss him.

"We can go anywhere." He tilted his head but kept his gaze pinned to mine.

"What?"

He threw his thumb over his shoulder. "Ms. Chiron said we could use the Academy grounds as inspiration for our project. I was thinking over near the stream."

I turned my head in the stream's direction so I didn't have to look at him. "That's kind of far. And down the hill."

And we'd be very much alone, I thought, but I didn't want to let him know.

It didn't matter because Knight began to pick up my things.

"I haven't said yes yet."

He stood and lowered his hand to me. "Is that what you want? For me to get on bended knee and ask you to come with me to a secluded spot so we can *work* together?" He winked.

Heat flooded between my legs. It wasn't a good idea to go off with Knight, to be alone with him. But that didn't stop my fingers from intertwining with his. As I stood and followed him past the tennis courts, toward the slope leading down the hill, I glanced back.

The only people looking our way were Briggs and Caleb. Did Knight tell them where he was going to take me?

I hesitated, and Knight glanced back. "What's wrong?"

"You told them, didn't you?" I jerked

my head toward his friends.

"Yes. Why wouldn't I?" He turned and placed his hand on my upper arm.

Despite the cotton of my shirt and the wool of my jacket separating his hand from my skin, his touch felt as if it were molten iron brandishing my skin with his mark.

"I don't understand why we need to be alone."

No matter how much my body reacted to his, I had never felt completely safe with him. Even when he had taken my virginity in the woods by Happy Pond, I wondered if he would leave me spent and alone, with nothing but dirt-caked clothes to keep me warm.

But he stayed. Only to use me for other reasons.

He sighed. "Fine. We will sit here and do our project."

Knight sat on the ground and looked up, waiting for me to follow his lead.

I nodded. "Okay. Good."

It was quiet here. More so than back where all the other kids were partnering up.

Knight leaned back on his elbows, stretched out his legs, and pointed to my brace. "Does it still hurt?"

"Not so much anymore. But when I put pressure on it, there's pain." I lightly kneaded my arm. "I have a doctor appointment tomorrow. She'll probably tell me I don't need the sling anymore."

He leaned on his right arm and reached over with his other, his finger trailing a line from my shoulder to my wrist.

"So, this doesn't hurt?"

My mouth went dry. I knew nothing would come out if I tried to utter any words. I shook my head.

"Mmm." His finger jumped, and a shiver ran through me as his fingernail lightly brushed the side of my knee.

He was taunting me.

My back faced the teacher and students. We were far enough away that they couldn't see or hear what was going on. And Knight took advantage of our distance.

"You should come back to my house . . . ."

I bit my lip, his fluttery touch becoming achingly unbearable as his fingers drifted farther up my thigh.

"No," I spat out.

His brows rose as well as the corner of his mouth. "Really?"

My right leg slid open. I wanted him to keep touching me; I wanted him to sink inside me. But that didn't mean I wanted to go home with him.

I shook my head. "I don't know."

His finger hooked into the seam of my panties, tugging them aside. I gasped as he slid two fingers over my wet folds.

I held back my intense moan. The boy

knew how to use his hands.

"I think you know, Violet. I think you've imagined me sneaking into your bedroom at night, flipping you over, and sinking my cock into your slippery wet pussy." Right as he said the last part, those fingers slid into my core.

God, I wanted my brace off now. I wanted to reach down and flick my clit as he finger-fucked me in the middle of class.

I tried to look back. Had anyone noticed us?

Knight read my mind. "No one has any idea what we're doing. We're too far away."

Though he tried to shift his hips so I wouldn't notice, his cock was bulging under his pants. That was why he wanted us to go down the hill. He wanted to fuck me.

My lips curled at the thought that I prevented him from getting everything he wanted.

His thumb circled my clit in the most delicious way, and I knew it wouldn't be long before I came. Would they hear? Would Knight believe he had won this tug of war with me?

I bit my lip to hold in my cries of pleasure as my climax slammed into me. I tried not to move, but it proved impossible. My head fell back, and I hoped someone mistook it for me enjoying the warm sun and not an orgasm from the devil.

As I came down from my euphoric high, he slid his hand out from between my legs. I watched with hooded eyes as he slipped them into his mouth, savoring my bliss.

My legs snapped shut. With a straightened back, I said, "We shouldn't have done that."

His fingers slowly slid out of his mouth. "You could have told me to stop at any time, Violet."

His fingers intertwined behind his head as he lay back, staring at the blue sky. Knight looked gorgeous, relaxed, and totally full of himself.

"It seems to me you do that a lot. You tell me to stay away, or you run off because you don't trust me, yet . . ." he turned his head, and his eyes slid up my body, sending shivers down to my still swollen clit, "when my fingers brush your skin, it's already on fire. You so easily melt into my touch."

My jaw ticked. He was right. I hated to admit it to myself, but Knight saw right through any protest I threw at him.

"I'm confused, that's all. I'm not purposely trying to be a tease."

And that was exactly what I'd been the whole time, wasn't it? I lifted my gaze, glancing over my shoulder to the class. A girl who said one thing to a boy and then did another. I used to hate those girls back at my old school; I thought they were full of it. But maybe they weren't . . .. Maybe they didn't want to like those boys.

I studied Knight for a moment. Extremely rich. Extremely handsome. Extremely confident. Too many extremes to count. But it was the one extreme that caused me to hesitate.

Knight King was extremely powerful, and he knew it.

"Then come back to my place. I promise to take care of you and your aunt."

Arabella's words from two days ago floated in my head. *Keep your friends close and your enemies closer.*

Was Knight my enemy? That was the confusing part.

I lifted my chin. "I can take care of myself."

His nose flared. "Goddamn it, Violet. I'm not saying you're weak . . .." He sat up to face me. "I'm saying my uncle is more powerful than you think. That little almost-gang rape I walked in on at the pool house last month was nothing compared to what he can do. I know he had a hand in my parents' death and the death of Jack Franklin."

"I know. You told me this before. Is there something new you learned?"

"Yes and no," he said with a sigh.

"What does that even mean?"

"I know someone who works with my uncle. I haven't found out anything that links my uncle to their deaths, but I found out who sent you those notes in your locker."

I swallowed, uncertain if I wanted to know the truth. I had a vague theory I hadn't told anyone, not even Arabella. But if I was right, then that meant one thing . . . .

"The notes came from my uncle's office. That thick stock is the same kind my uncle uses at the mayor's office. And his assistant had delivered a few letters to the school. Violet, this was what I meant when I said you were in danger."

I had to stay with Knight. My theory was correct, and Knight would be the only one who could keep the mayor away from me.

I took a steady breath. "Okay, I'll move back into your home."

The breath came out in a gust. Deflated. Knight had me. He could protect me. But how long would it be until he turned his devilish gaze on me?

NINE

Violet

"I DON'T THINK THEY serve dinner here, Violet," Arabella noted as she stared at the inked drawings plastered all over the wall. Hundreds of pictures. Some sweet, like cherubs, and others not so angelic, like a skull ripped open with brains inside.

I told Knight I'd move in with him yesterday but wanted to wait for the weekend to do it. I needed to let Arabella know I was moving out of her place. I planned to break it to her over dinner tonight.

I was worried how she would take it. After all, she didn't trust Knight either.

My fingers curled around the locket I had around my neck. It held my baby picture and it was one of the few connections, other than my bracelet, I had connecting me to my old life.

As I stared up at the shop walls I smiled. I hadn't been here before but it too felt like a connection to my old life.

"We're not here to get dinner. I need to speak to someone, and then we can head over to Jack's Place."

Her eyes slid toward the back, and she leaned closer to me. "I don't think we're welcome here."

I turned my head and saw Drew

narrow her eyes at me. Her long black hair was pulled back into a French braid, and she wore a sleeveless black T-shirt and jeans. Black work boots that went up mid-calf rattled with chains hanging in the lace loops as she took a step closer.

"It's me . . .. She hates me."

Arabella pulled at my black wool jacket, and I turned to face her.

"Then let's leave," Arabella whispered.

"Violet." I heard a voice call me from behind.

Spinning on my heels, I found Jewel sashaying out from the back, nudging Drew aside.

Jewel was sporting a black and white-striped tank that exposed her midriff and blue leggings. Tattoos covered her shoulders and slid down her back until they disappeared under her tank.

"Hey, Jewel." I nodded, shoving my hands into my pockets.

Jewel's eyes shifted to Arabella and not

in a welcoming way.

"This is my friend, Arabella. She's been helping me out."

Jewel's eyes slid down Arabella's body with scrutiny. "She want a tat?" Jewel waved at the wall. "Since she's your friend, I can knock ten percent off anything from this wall."

She pointed to the wall with the small cutesy tattoos—nothing but hearts and cartoon characters and symbols.

"I'm not really a tat sort of girl."

Jewel's brow furrowed. "Not even a tramp stamp?"

I rolled my lips over my teeth to stop from laughing. I could tell Jewel was fucking with Arabella, and my friend fell for it.

"So generous, but no." She glanced around and saw the nicked pine bench. "I'll just wait here. Check my stats on HitLoc." She held up her phone.

"Right. You do that." Jewel nodded and

waved me to follow her.

I walked toward the back as Drew's eyes locked on me.

"Never mind her." Jewel held up a black curtain that led to a small room. "She's mad that I'm talking to a Northie."

I hadn't even lived in North Green Hills for two months, and they already saw me as a Northie.

"I'm not from North Green Hills—"

"It doesn't matter." She shook her head. "You live there now. Besides, who gives a fuck what others think? North or South, they just want someone to hate. So they point their finger, and if you are far enough away or dress a little different, talk a little different, then that gives them the excuse to unleash their hate."

Now it was my turn to assess her. For a woman close to my mom's age, still dealing drugs, she was pretty smart. Smarter than most people I had met.

There was a small, nicked metal desk

that I couldn't tell if they painted it green or gray. Jewel sat on a pine chair in front of the old beat-up desk.

I glanced around to look at the art on the walls. There were more pictures of tattoos, but these had greater detail and were framed. Some were photographs of customers after they had completed their work, while some were framed close-ups of just the tattoo.

Other than the desk and pictures, there wasn't much else.

I heard a creaking sound and saw Jewel close a desk drawer. She placed a black device on the table and slid it toward me.

"What's this?"

"A phone. My cousin's old phone. Once he was flush with money from staying away from the bus, he gave me his old one. Told me he didn't need it anymore. He bought a new phone, no more used shit for him."

I lifted it and noticed its heft. After

tapping at it, the phone lit up. "Why would I want his phone?"

She leaned back in the chair, resting her hands on her stomach. "It's what's inside it. Emails sent from a sera.hill@Hillingham.com. I don't know who that is, but the email talks about the bus heading to Winter Rivers University. I figured that might interest you."

My fingers curled tighter around the phone as if she were about to ask for it back.

"What do you want for it?"

There was always a price. I knew enough to expect it. She may have liked my mom, but it didn't mean she would throw me a bone for free.

"Get me into Green Hills Academy after hours. This coming Tuesday."

My eyes widened. "I-I can't do that—"

"Maybe not," she shrugged, "but your friend can."

I glanced back, unable to see past the

black curtain. "How do you know that?"

"I know lots of things. The point is, what's on that phone could help you, and I need into the school when no one is around."

"You won't do anything . . . something that might hurt people?"

She stood and moved around the desk toward the curtain. "Don't you worry about that. No one will be harmed." Her lips twitched with a brief grin.

I swallowed and studied the black phone in my hand. If there was an email from Seraphina on it, what other information could be there that would prove the accident was more than faulty brakes?

Seraphina had been unusually friendly to me lately, and I knew, deep in my gut, it had something to do with that bus.

"Fine. I'll make it happen."

I hated promising something that only Arabella could deliver, but I needed the phone.

Jewel showed me back out, and I grabbed Arabella, who was happy to leave. I tucked my arm into hers and pulled her close once we were outside on the sidewalk.

"Arabella . . . promise you won't be mad?"

"Ugh, you sold me to that Jewel chick, and now I'm her slave, didn't you?"

I tilted my head. "What? No. Don't be ridiculous." I slapped her lightly on her shoulder.

"I am being serious. I got a very black-market, human pets vibe from that place. Maybe it was just that the other chick—"

"Drew. The one who didn't go in the back with me was Drew."

"Yeah, Drew kept staring at me the whole time. And not a curious sort of stare. The creepy, I'm-going-to-chop-you-up-into-little-bits kind of glare. I pretended like I was checking my phone, but really, I had my fingers hovering over the emergency call button just in case."

"Oh my god, you're such a wuss." I chuckled as we kept walking arm in arm down the street.

"Hey, I grew up in North Green Hills. I can't help if I'm a product of my environment. I'm a spoiled history nerd, and I'm not afraid to admit it. I know what I am, and I'm sure they do too."

I shrugged. "At least you own it."

"And you've had the fortunate experience of living in both worlds—theirs and mine. I can't even say that for myself."

I nibbled my lips. "It's funny you should say that . . .. What if I told you there was a way you could help me with my old world?"

She sighed. "I knew it. You want me to be a drug mule for them. Look, I don't mind the occasional dick up my asshole for sexual purposes, but nothing else.

Well, no . . . maybe a dildo."

"Oh, god, too much information." I made a gagging sound. "Seriously, though, it has nothing to do with drugs or anything in any part of your body, Arabella. Just getting into the school after hours."

She stopped, and I almost fell backward as we were still arm and arm. "That's what you want me to help you with? Getting you into the school at night?"

"Not me. Jewel. I don't know why, but she promised it wasn't to hurt anyone. She probably wants to leave something in a kid's locker who owes her money," I said and hoped Arabella bought it.

I had a feeling it was much worse than scaring someone to pay up. Jewel didn't appear like a person who needed to threaten anyone—just owing money to her would be threat enough.

"Sure, that won't be a problem. But if she gets caught, I don't know her."

I nodded. "Jewel knows not to snitch."

I glanced around the road. The Italian restaurant I wanted to take Arabella to was still two blocks away.

"There's something else, isn't there?" Arabella asked with concern on her features.

"What do you mean?"

"You've been gnawing on your lower lip so much today, I worried you've been attempting a DIY lip enhancement surgery."

I scrunched up my face. "Whatever."

"Seriously, Violet. You know you can tell me anything." She held my hand between hers.

"Okay, but please don't be mad."

"Of course I won't be mad. Just be honest with me."

I nodded. She was right. I had wanted honesty from Knight for so long and rarely got it. It was only fair I told Arabella the truth.

"The note that was in my locker on the

first day and then the one I got right before I was arrested . . . They were from the mayor."

She gasped and pulled away from me, covering her mouth. "Shit."

"Knight figured it out. He knows someone who works with the mayor. I'm worried that the mayor wants to silence me for that."

And maybe even more. From what I was gathering from Knight, the mayor would never have taken me in just for appearance's sake. He wanted something from me before the potential rape ever happened.

"I hate to say this, Violet, since you don't trust Knight, but maybe you are safer with him. You two share an enemy—the mayor."

I nodded. "Yeah, that's what I wanted to talk to you about. I plan to move back into Knight's place this Friday. I'm sorry."

She wrapped her arms around me.

"Don't be. I'd rather see you safe. And if that means you can't live with me, then so be it."

I forced a smile on my face and wondered—and not for the first time—if I was really safe under Knight's roof?

TEN

Violet

THE SUN WAS BRIGHT with warm autumn rays beaming down. The vivid blue sky was in sharp contrast with the red leaves floating around in the cool breeze.

I inhaled. Hints of smoke, earth, and dread filled my nostrils. It was Friday, and

I stood waiting in front of the school while Arabella grabbed something she forgot in her car.

Today was the day I moved back into Knight's home. Instead of going to see the latest comic franchise movie with Arabella, I was packing my stuff and my aunt's stuff to get out of Arabella's home.

My aunt had stopped her lease on her apartment once Knight let her move into his place several weeks ago. When I left Knight's place, Aunt Dahlia had to go with me.

I hated pulling her all over the town, but it was too dangerous to leave her somewhere all alone. I never thought I would be the one protecting her.

"Got it. Thanks for waiting," Arabella said, slightly winded as she pushed her backpack up on her shoulder.

"Can't be a proper student without a

backpack," I said jokingly.

"I don't know. I feel like with everything being digital now, why do we even need a backpack? My theory is within the next decade, they'll become obsolete. Then after a few decades, they'll come back in style like how something vintage becomes trendy again."

"My god, you're a nerd. Is this what you think about all day?" I giggled as we passed through the front door being held open by the school attendants.

"Yes. You have no idea all the crazy shit I got jam-packed up in here." She pointed to her brain. "Anyway, I'm heading to the library for first period. I usually have history, but we are allowed to work on our senior project."

That was why she was following me to my locker; it was near the library. We climbed the steps and strolled down the hall, weaving in and out of other kids.

"Does every class have a senior project? I got teamed up with Knight in art class for a project too."

She nodded and leaned against the locker next door as I set about unlocking mine.

"Yes. Senior year here is a joke. By this point, everyone knows where they're going to college, and all the parents care about is making sure the kids get good grades so they can graduate with high GPAs."

I opened my locker and gasped. Inside, there was an envelope. I grasped the envelope with trembling fingers.

"Oh no," Arabella said as she saw what I pulled out. "Let me have that." She plucked it from my fingers before I could answer.

The envelope was made from

different paper—not as thick and had a light pink color instead of the cream. Maybe the mayor found out Knight had been asking about the envelopes I was receiving, and he switched it up. Maybe he was trying to fool me.

But it wouldn't work.

Arabella slipped her finger under the flap and tore it until it was open. The air filled with metallic confetti. At first, I thought it was anthrax or something poisonous and jumped back. But within seconds, I realized it was glitter—harmless, though still the herpes of the crafting world.

"For a threat, it sure smells nice," Arabella noted.

I sniffed the air and noticed it smelled of jasmine. *That's weird.*

She pulled out the letter and opened it. Her eyes rounded. "Holy shit . . ."

I frowned and felt the tears threatening to fall. "What . . . what does it say?"

Her gaping mouth broke into an enormous smile as she handed me the letter. "Seraphina just invited you to her eighteenth birthday party. Can you fucking believe it?"

My tears dried up instantly as confusion wrinkled my face. I took the letter and gazed at the gold inlaid typeface. My fingers slid over the beveled letters. The invitation had been handmade, not cheap, and printed using a laser printer.

"Okay, something is wrong here. It's one thing to be forced to sit with her at lunch and listen to her babble about the latest celebrity breakup and how the royals have gone to shit, but having to go to her birthday party . . .? No," I shook my head and pushed the invitation to Arabella, "this is where I draw the line. I will not spend a dime buying that bitch a gift."

As I gazed up at Arabella, expecting to discover understanding, I was shocked at what I saw. My friend was shaking her head. She disagreed with me.

"No, Violet, you have to go. I mean, this right here," she waved her hand around the invite as if she were a game show hostess from the 1970s, "is a royal invitation. Do you know how epic Seraphina's parties are? They make the Oscar parties look weak."

My head shot back. "Who are you, and what have you done with my friend? Is this payback for me going to live with Knight? Is this some sort of passive-aggressive hate?"

"Do me a favor. Take this invite, hold it to your chest and turn to face the students walking by."

"Weird," I mumbled but did as she said.

Once I turned with the jasmine-scented letter plastered to my chest, I noticed all eyes shifted in my direction. They flickered from the invite to my face and back again. Some of them whispered to each other and pointed at me, while others plastered on fake grins and waved at me as if they were desperate for me to notice them.

That was when I realized what had happened. With a little piece of expensive paper, I was popular. I officially became part of the bitch crew.

All at once, I felt utter joy and revulsion. Like that little girl in me who wanted to be a princess finally got her wish, only to discover it was to be the princess of Hell.

"This is so fucked-up," I said as I stared

at the students.

"Isn't it, though? Don't you see why you have to go?"

"No." I turned to face her, shoving the invite back into my locker. "I don't see. I don't want to be accepted by Seraphina. I don't like her, and I wish she'd stop trying to be my friend."

Arabella groaned and grabbed my upper arms. Even with my brace off, there was still a slight ache by my shoulder when she gripped me.

"I get that, I do, but think outside the box with this. At first, I thought Seraphina was just doing it to make her mom happy. I assumed her mom told her to make nice in public to ward off any legal problems you might throw their way."

"Yeah, I think that's the reason too."

"That might be some of it, but I believe there's more going on here. Seraphina knows something about you. I don't know what, but it must be something big. Something so big, she would invite you to her birthday party."

I snorted. "It's a fucking birthday party. I know you said it was like the Oscars, but really—"

"Not like the Oscars. *Better* than any Oscar party. There are A-list celebrities who would do anything for an invitation to one of her parties."

I rolled my eyes. "That's not true."

Arabella stepped back and sighed. She pulled her backpack around and dug through it until she lifted out her phone. After a few taps, she showed me what she found. "That's her party from last year."

My eyes bulged. I grabbed the phone out of her hand and held it up to my face. "But that's—"

"Antonio Silva."

My head rose, and I stared at Arabella in disbelief. "She got the star of *High School Hero* to come to her party?"

Arabella smirked. "She didn't have to get him. I bet his agent begged for an invite. And Seraphina invited him. And if you look over his shoulder—" She pointed down at the phone.

"Oh my god, that's Celina Harwich. *The* Celina Harwich. At twelve years old, she was the youngest person to win a Grammy."

"Yeah, but that was five years ago. And she's won a Grammy every year since."

A sense of dread washed over me as what Arabella was telling me sank in. I had been invited to the hottest party of the year.

"I have nothing to wear to her birthday party," I mumbled in a daze.

"She usually has a theme. That's how

you know what to wear." Arabella reached behind me and pulled out the invite from my locker.

After studying it, she said, "The theme is 80s prom. So, you don't even need to spend a lot on a dress."

I tilted my head. "But wouldn't she notice? I'm sure the people invited to this are spending tons on their outfits."

She handed me the invite and sighed. "That's the thing about the super-rich. They don't need to flaunt their money by buying the most expensive things for every occasion. Sometimes they enjoy slumming it; you know, buying cheap stuff for entertainment. Like this party. I am betting Seraphina will probably wear some cheap, tacky taffeta dress or one of those gold lamé dresses that were big in the 80s."

I nodded, absorbing what she was

telling me. When I glanced down at the invitation again, I gasped. "Oh shit, this is tomorrow. It's on Saturday."

Arabella smiled. "Well, it looks like instead of packing tonight, we'll be roaming thrift stores for old 80s dresses. And whatever you do, don't lose the invite, or you won't get in. I've heard there's something in the invitation that they scan or check, so it can't be duplicated. Only one per person."

I nodded and made sure to tuck the invitation into my backpack.

It sounded like fun, but I rubbed my chest as it tickled with a sense of dread. What Arabella had said a few minutes ago made sense.

Seraphina knew something so big about me, she was willing to be friends with me and invite me to her exclusive bash. A month ago, she hated everything about me, but something had changed. And maybe this party was the perfect opportunity for me to find out what was different.

ELEVEN

Knight

"Where have you been?" I asked as I watched Violet move through the entranceway to the house. She had a cheap white garment bag hanging on one arm and a suitcase in the other.

She glared at me. "No, please, I don't

need any help."

Normally, I enjoyed when she was being snarky, but not tonight.

I rolled my shoulders and walked over, lifting both bags from her. She turned to head out of the house before I stepped in front of her.

"Hey, I asked you a question. Where have you been? You missed dinner."

Her head reared back. "Sorry, *Dad.*"

I placed the suitcase on the ground and grabbed her arm. "This needs to stop. I'm helping you, and you're acting as if you're being forced to be here."

She yanked her arm back, rubbing where I had touched her. My grip had been light, so I knew she wasn't in pain. I would never hurt her.

"Aren't I, though? Last I checked, I never wanted to live here. Never wanted to come to North Green Hills Academy. But your uncle took me in and lied to me, to my aunt, and to everyone. So, here I am.

Forgive me if I'm not dancing on clouds to be under this roof once again."

There were footsteps, and I glanced over to find my new butler, Carter, coming to grab Violet's things. I handed over the garment bag.

Once he left, I gazed at Violet. "I understand this isn't ideal. I'd rather be spending my Friday nights out partying with my friends instead of going over any of my uncle's documents that might help me find out if he killed my parents. Nothing about this is normal or wanted, but here we are."

She hugged herself. "This sucks."

"Yes, it does." I stepped forward and tucked some locks of her brunette hair behind her ear. "But at least we have each other."

Her golden-brown eyes gazed up at me, searching my face. "I want to believe you, Knight. But I have so many unanswered questions." She lifted her hands and placed them on my chest. The feel of her skin jolted my heart.

"I hate this," I whispered as I nuzzled my nose into her hair and pulled her close. "I just want to get my uncle. Expose him for what he's done. And then you walk into my world, and in the process, I do things I never would have done."

Her arms slip through mine, and she fists my T-shirt. "Like what?"

"Like letting you meet Ava. Telling you what happened to my parents. Making sure Seraphina was punished for locking you in that bus. You're my distraction."

Her head pressed against my chest, and I heard her inhale. My cock twitched, knowing she wanted me as much as I wanted her.

"Was it you who kept her from getting into Winter Rivers University?" She glanced up, and all I wanted to do was fall into the pools of her eyes.

"Yes."

She smirked. "Does it make me a terrible person that I enjoyed watching her find out?"

"No."

My mind flew to earlier in the week when I saw Seraphina with Violet. "Why are you hanging out with Seraphina?"

Her shoulders slumped, and she let out a groan. Violet pulled away, and I had the feeling she hoped I wouldn't bring it up.

"It's strange . . .. I don't understand it much myself. It started last week when Arabella and I ran into Seraphina and her mom shopping at the mall."

"Mrs. Hillington?"

She nodded. "Yeah, Crystal. She kept making nice to us while Seraphina just wanted to leave. It was obvious her mom liked us, but Seraphina didn't. So much so, she paid for my clothes and then bought us lunch."

The hairs on the back of my neck rose as I scratched my chin. "Crystal. You said

Crystal, right? I mean, I knew her name, but it didn't click until you said it."

Violet frowned. "Yeah, Crystal. Why is her first name so important?"

I entangled my fingers with hers and pulled her toward the stairs. "Let me show you something. I ran into her at a coffee shop earlier this week. Not that she knew why I was there . . .." I stopped at the top of the stairs as a thought popped into my head.

"Knight? You alright?"

A few pieces of my uncle's puzzle were falling into place. I wanted to tell Violet, but I wondered if her new-found friendship with Seraphina might prove useful. If Violet knew she was being used to get something from Seraphina, she might not agree to do it.

"Yes. Just realized we still need to come up with an art project to work on. We were so distracted the other day when we got our assignment."

Violet's cheeks turned pink, and I knew thoughts of the orgasm I gave her were dancing in her head.

"Maybe on Sunday. We can work on it then," she said before nibbling on her lip.

As much as I wanted to slam her body against the wall and nestle my cock between her thighs, I had to show her what my uncle's assistant gave me.

"Come to my bedroom." I waved for her to follow.

Her blush grew deeper. "Okay."

I couldn't help but smile. I knew what she was thinking, and I wanted that too, but that wasn't why I was inviting to her to my bedroom.

Once we were inside my bedroom, I shut the door. I watched Violet as she awkwardly made her way toward my overstuffed leather chair near the bookcase. Then she glimpsed the window and moved in that direction. I walked over to my desk and got out my device.

Turning it on and pulling out the antenna, I swept the room.

"What are you doing?" she asked, her fingers sliding over the blue silk curtains.

I lifted my finger to my lips to signal for her to be quiet. The small black device lit up once I swept my bookcase.

I reached behind a few books and found it. Opening the window, I walked out onto my balcony and threw it.

"What was that?" Violet came up behind me, her hand reaching up and warming my shoulder.

"A listening device. A bug. There might be a few more in my room. Wait here while I find them."

Her eyes grew, but she nodded and stayed on the balcony. It took me a few minutes, but I found two more. Once I got rid of them, I waved Violet back inside.

"Did your uncle do that?"

"Yeah. It's a regular thing now. Whenever I come home from school or from hanging out with Briggs and Caleb, I find a new bug. Either someone on my staff is planting them, or someone is breaking in while I'm gone."

She slapped her forehead. "Man, that's fucked-up."

"That's the Kings." I smirked as I made my way to my desk and placed my finger on the lowest drawer. After a few seconds, there was a click, and it popped open.

"Did you just—"

"I had the desk specially made. The bottom drawer is reinforced steel and as secure as a safe. It also uses my fingerprint to unlock. No one can get into this drawer but me."

She strolled over, and I watched her hips sway as she came close. The air filled with vanilla and made my mouth water.

I reached for her, unable to keep my hands away, but then she asked, "What's this?"

The emails. Should I show her or wait

until I tugged down her jeans and let my cock answer her question?

It had been so long since I fucked her . . . but I guessed I could wait a little longer.

"These are my uncle's emails. He thought he deleted them, but I have someone in his office who makes copies of everything for me. Even things from years ago."

"Is that Seraphina's mom?"

"Yes, that's why I kept saying her name downstairs. It finally clicked for me. The Hillingham company. Sure, they own lots of subsidiaries, but it's Seraphina's father who owns them. That is his company. But these emails aren't from Mr. Hillingham; they're from Mrs. Hillingham. She invested in the Franklin First drug."

Violet shrugged. "So?"

"She invested after the drug failed. It was supposed to be a potential cure for certain cancers, but it failed phase one. The FDA couldn't approve it. Why was she investing? Why was my uncle investing?"

Violet leaned against the desk, her gaze drifting across the room as she was deep in thought.

"I wish I knew. But . . ." She gasped and pushed off the desk. "The phone. I don't know how much info it would have, but it might help."

I tilted my head. "Phone?"

"You're not the only one with connections," she said as the corner of her lip curled.

She shuffled out of the room, and I followed. Violet went down the hall and pushed open her bedroom door.

Carter had brought up her bags and placed them at the foot of her bed. She threw her black suitcase on top of the cream-colored duvet on her bed.

Once her suitcase was open, she dug in the side and pulled out an outdated black phone. It had to be at least three years old.

"I think I need to get you a new phone,"

I commented as I studied the bulky thing in her hand.

"It's not mine. It's the bus driver's old phone. The one who wasn't around when I got locked in and the brakes *supposedly* malfunctioned. The same driver who was still not around when the bus rolled out of Winter River's parking lot."

"How did you get that?" I reached out, but Violet held the phone away.

"Nope. This is mine. What I've found on here is interesting." She twisted her lips and stared at me, waiting for my response.

I stepped toward her, slipped my hand around her waist, and pulled her flush against my body. She gasped. I guessed she expected me to get down on my knees and beg for the phone.

She had no idea it would happen the other way around. I'd have her on her knees, offering the phone, just so she could suck my cock.

Nuzzling my nose into the curve of her

neck, I took a little nibble. Violet moaned and melted into my arms.

Hearing her like that made me want more. Sliding my hand down, I cupped her ass, pushing her onto my hardening, jean-covered cock.

"You like to tease me, don't you?" I lifted my head and stared into her softening eyes.

She bit her lip. "Maybe."

"I don't like to be teased." I reached up and slid my fingers through her tangled hair, pulling her back. Her nose flared, but her tits jutted out as she arched her back.

Violet liked a little pain, and I intended to let her have it.

"Now, on your knees and suck my cock."

TWELVE

Violet

KNIGHT LIGHTLY PULLED TO help in case I hadn't heard him. He wanted me on my knees, licking his cock like a lollipop.

He thought it was a punishment for me. He had no idea I had rubbed my clit to that fantasy countless times. Imagining what he'd taste like and how he'd sound as I swirled my tongue around him.

I reached for his jeans as I lowered to the ground, but he waved me off.

"I do it," Knight said as if it was a lesson I needed to learn. From here on out, if he presented me with his cock, that was when I'd open my mouth in acceptance.

I placed the phone on the floor by my knees and eagerly waited. He took his time too. The hypocrite. He hated to be teased, but he sure didn't mind doing it to me.

My mouth was watering.

The pull of his zipper fly was torturously slow, but it wasn't all torment. Once the fly was open, he lifted his hands and pulled off his T-shirt, tossing it across the room. His ripped abs were a treat for my eyes to feast on. I had no idea what he did to achieve those chiseled muscles, but whatever it was, he should never stop.

Then he pushed. Hooking his thumbs into his jeans, tugging them down. After a few lifts of his legs, he got them down enough to kick them to the side.

Knight King stood before me naked, and he was every girl's fantasy. Bad boy, killer body, and knew how to fuck.

He slid his hand back into my hair while the other curled around the base of his cock, guiding me to it. I could already see the precum, and once he got to my lips, he painted them for me.

"Open your mouth and take me, Violet."

Silly boy. He didn't have to ask. I was already licking the creamy lipstick he gave me as my eyes focused on the prize. My lips puckered, kissing the tip, and then I licked. He tasted like the best salty treat, and I couldn't stop with just one lick.

My hands settled on his thighs, thick and taut, so I didn't fall over as I leaned forward. I gazed up to discover Knight's jaw twitching as he stared at me. When I opened fully and sucked him inside my mouth, that was when I heard him groan.

"Fuck, Violet. That's it." His voice grew deep as his grip tightened in my hair.

His other hand flexed, stroking his cock, following my lips. Knight tasted better than I had expected. Yes, there was that usual spicy flavor, but there was also something more. It was uniquely Knight, and I loved it.

My fingers dug into his thighs as I squirmed. My panties were already wet as he slid over my tongue.

Knight sucked in a breath between clenched teeth. "Violet. I didn't expect you to be so fucking good at this."

Right as I was about to pull him in deeper, he pushed me back. My lips throbbing and wet, I stared up at him in confusion.

"Get up," he demanded as he worked his cock.

"Is something—" I tried to ask as I stood, but he cut me off.

His hands flew to the hem of my shirt, pulling so hard I heard a rip. I lifted my arms, a lingering twinge of pain in my shoulder from the accident, and within seconds, my shirt was on the ground.

His steely gray gaze ate me up as if I weren't wearing a bra and a pair of jeans.

He pointed to my jeans. "Those need to be off."

It wasn't an order but a threat, and my clit twitched in wonder at what punishment he'd dole out if I lingered. So much heat and anger laced his words. I wondered if what I did to his cock caused him to lose control—and Knight wasn't the type of guy who enjoyed control slipping from his grasp.

Once I tugged my jeans off, I continued to undress without his direction. My pink panties and matching bra formed a heap on the floor. I had a feeling Knight wouldn't stop me. He stood there slowly stroking his cock; his eyes focused more on the clothes leaving my body than what I hid underneath.

He walked over to where his jeans were and lifted out a condom from his pocket. As he strolled back to me, tossing the wrapper aside, he rolled down the condom.

"Why are you still standing?" he asked, not even glancing up at me.

It was a question that required no answer. I scurried over to the bed and sat.

Knight stood about a foot in front of me. His heated gaze meandered down my body like molten metal. My clit throbbed. I rubbed my thighs, trying to ease the intensity, but nothing helped.

"You need to learn, Violet. When I'm about to fuck you, that means your clothes come off and legs spread wide. I won't say it again." He still had not moved closer.

The only reason my legs were closed was because I didn't want him to see how wet I was. It was different when we were in the woods at night—he hadn't noticed that I was practically dripping with need.

But now it was daylight. We were in a bedroom, and all I had to do was pull my legs apart and show him my soaked pussy.

His brow rose in question. I was taking too long. With a fortifying breath, I opened my legs. With my eyes raised toward the ceiling, I leaned back on my elbows. I couldn't bring myself to watch his expression change.

Would he be disappointed? Disgusted?

It wasn't like my mom had The Talk with me. Most of what I learned about sex was through my friends and overhearing guys. But they never mentioned how wet girls were when they got turned on. Maybe it was just me.

I flinched when I felt his fingers brush my thighs.

"My god, you're beautiful, Violet."

His words surprised me, and I glanced over at him. Knight was staring between my thighs. Did he like that?

"I'm so wet," I mumbled with a frown.

He smiled and nodded, not taking his eyes off my throbbing pussy. His hand moved toward my apex, and I watched as his thumb slid over my folds. I moaned loud and long at the bolt of pleasure that erupted.

Knight lifted his thumb to his lips and sucked. "And you're delicious."

Realizing he enjoyed the taste of me felt empowering. That I had something he wanted. My legs fell back a little further because I wanted him to see me now. I wanted to show him how wet he made me.

He lowered his hand again, slipping two fingers into my core. It felt amazing, and I moved my hips, but it wasn't enough.

"Look at you. So greedy," he said with a smirk.

He tried to pretend like it didn't affect him, but I saw how quickly his chest moved with heavy breaths. How his eyes glazed over as he watched his hand fuck me.

"I guess you want more?" he asked.

I nodded and lifted my hand to my tit, rubbing and pinching my nipple. I noticed his other hand slid over his balls, squeezing and tugging.

My head fell back when his thumb swiped over my clit. A moan escaped my lips as pleasure spread throughout my body.

Within moments, I felt his cock thrust inside me. A little at first, but I could barely catch my breath before he had filled me. I looked up when he hadn't moved.

Knight stood there at the edge of the bed, my leg hooked on his arm. His eyes closed, nose flared, he looked like an ancient Greek statue.

After some time, his hips swayed. Heat surged, and I moved my hips to catch its charge.

When he finally opened his eyes, I noticed something there. It differed from anything I had ever seen from him before. Softer. As if he was opening up to me and his eyes were the door.

My heart hammered in my chest. Was this more than a fuck to him? I had assumed that was what he wanted from me—information and a good fuck.

Knight had been right that the mayor wanted me for some reason, that I was important to him. And since Knight wanted to know everything about his uncle, I thought that was the only reason he kept me around.

Maybe it was more than that.

I shook my head. It was the euphoria from sex. The intensity clouded my judgment. I was a good fuck for him, nothing more.

He fell on top of me, and my legs wrapped around his waist, holding him close. I heard him grunt as his teeth nibbled my neck while he surged in and out of me.

This was how I had always pictured sex. Bodies hugging one another, an epic embrace of emotion and erotic pleasure.

Knight rose onto his elbows and gazed at me with hooded eyes. They slid to my lips, and without hesitation, his mouth fell to mine.

The kiss was deep and passionate as my core tightened around him. It wouldn't be long before I came, but a part of me didn't want that.

I hoped this would last forever. A perfect mix of carnal pleasure and emotional high.

Our kiss broke, and he nibbled his way to my earlobe.

"Come for me, my little flower."

My eyes shut, and my head reared back as I let out a cry. My climax hit me suddenly. I felt his fingers in my hair, pulling as he rutted into me. He tightened his grip and grunted out my name.

After a few moments, his body slackened. My limbs felt like rubber. Knight pulled out of me, turned, and sat on the bed.

We were both out of breath, and his skin shone with perspiration. I tried to get up, but it was no use. Instead, I rolled back until my legs were fully on the bed. Knight came over and pulled me close, cradling me.

It was nice and not at all like Knight. He never struck me as the cuddling type.

And with that thought, whatever tender cocoon I had imagined in our shared moment disintegrated.

I sighed as he nuzzled the back of my neck.

"Does that tickle?" He never stopped as he asked.

"No, it feels good."

"You seem tense. People usually relax after a good fuck."

I sighed once again.

"Is something wrong?" He stiffened. "Should I go?"

Shifting until I was facing Knight, I placed my hand on his damp chest. Even now, I felt the heat grow between my legs as my fingers danced along his muscles.

There was no denying that we had a connection. But he had built a wall around himself long before I entered his life, and I worried I'd never be able to breach it.

"Maybe?" I shrugged.

It wasn't much of an answer, but my head and heart were battling it out. The aftermath left me confused.

His brows shot up. "Maybe? Uh, okay." Knight blinked and stared past my shoulder. After a minute, he sat up and turned his back to me. "I guess now that you live in the house, I don't need to stay with you." Knight tilted his head to the side, waiting for my reaction.

My eyes burned. He wanted an out.

Seraphina was right. I was just a fuck for him, someone he could use to taunt his uncle.

He knew all this wasn't easy for me—coming to live here and having my world turned upside down. Even though I shouldn't have been surprised Knight was incapable of understanding I required time, I was.

Maybe it was better if he went.

"I'm perfectly capable of taking care of myself. You can go." I rolled over, never looking at him.

The bed shifted as he stood. I glimpsed him picking up the phone from the floor, the one I got from Jewel. "I'm taking this."

I let him. I had already searched the various texts and emails. There was only one I found from what appeared to be Seraphina's email. It was vague, and there wasn't much I could do with it. Maybe Knight would have better luck than me.

He wordlessly grabbed his stuff and

left. As much as I told him to go, my heart ached when I heard the bedroom door close behind him.

THIRTEEN

Violet

"**Are you sure you** won't come in? I don't think anyone would notice," I said as I stared at Arabella.

She sat with her hands on the steering wheel and a frown on her face. "I'd love to. Just to see how wild the party was, but I wasn't invited to Seraphina's birthday bash; you were."

I glanced over at the Hillingham's gigantic mansion. It obviously cost them a lot of money but looked wildly out of place in the mountains of the East Coast, with its Spanish tiled roof and stucco walls—not to mention the two large palm trees framing the entrance.

I turned back and grabbed her hand. "Then come. I don't think—"

My door flew open, and a man stood there holding out his hand. "Invitation."

"Oh, uh, just a second." I grabbed the purse Arabella let me borrow because I had never owned one before. It wasn't like I had credit cards and keys to cars to carry around. What I had either went into my backpack or my pockets.

I dug around the bag and pulled out the slightly wrinkled invitation, holding it up for him.

He plucked it from my fingers and

took a moment to examine. "Ms. Adler?"

"Yes."

"The party is through that door."

I saw where he was waving and noticed another set of large doors that I thought was a garage.

"Okay." I stepped out and was about to turn back to say goodbye to Arabella when he shut the door for me.

"But I wanted to—"

"Your driver can wait for you out on the street," he said as he pointed to the doors of the house once again. The man wore a black hoodie and dark jeans, with a black coiled earpiece, and he wasn't too happy I was still standing next to him.

I watched Arabella drive off as another car pulled up. There was a line of Bentleys and various sports cars curving down the driveway and spilling out into the street.

My tongue slipped into the spot of the missing tooth—a nervous habit I had picked up. I made my way toward the doors and wondered if I could even afford to fix my tooth? I had always been on my aunt's dental plan growing up, but now that I was eighteen, I probably wouldn't be covered.

I shook my head. Now wasn't the time to wonder about dentists. I had to spend the night pretending I belonged in a crowd of millionaires.

There was a couple in front of me. One wore a neon pink dress, while the guy wore a white suit with a black button-up shirt and black- and white-checkered tie. His hair was teased and bigger than hers.

I followed them, assuming they knew where they were going. There was a small door to the side of what I had thought was the garage, and they went through it. That must have been what the parking attendant meant.

Opening the door, I stepped through into darkness. I heard music, 80s stuff. I think it was "Girls Just Wanna Have Fun", but it sounded muffled, like it was coming from deeper inside the home.

I blinked a few times, and my eyes finally adjusted. Suddenly I saw a bright white set of teeth only inches from my face.

"Hello. Welcome to the prom," the teeth said.

"What the fuck?" I asked with a gasp.

"Black light. Totally awesome, for sure," the teeth mentioned.

"Totally," I mumbled.

"So, here's your prom goody bag." She held up something, and I saw the outline as my eyes adjusted. As I stared at her, I noticed the outline of her face became clearer. She had a side ponytail and wouldn't stop smiling at me like it was her job to be bubbly and happy.

Super creepy.

I grabbed the bag, and it had heft. The handles were a thick chain—apparently no cheap paper party bags for Seraphina.

"Thanks."

"Just head through the door in the corner and dance like you just don't care!"

As I walked, a door appeared. The black light idea was terrible. I could barely see, and I wouldn't be surprised if a drunk guest fell and tried to sue Seraphina. I suspected the type of people she invited to these things thought taking someone to court was as natural as breathing.

I was relieved to discover normal lighting once I opened the door. It was a hallway with marble tile and white walls. As I decided which way to turn, I noticed the music was coming from my left, so I headed in that direction.

As I made my way down the hall, I examined my party bag. It was an actual purse. And I wasn't sure, but it looked like it was made of leather.

I came to a stop before I left the hallway and opened the bag. There was so much stuff in there. It had jewelry, makeup, a bath bomb that smelled amazing, and a bunch of stuff I had to open to find out what it was.

"This is crazy," I mumbled to myself.

"No, it's vintage Chanel," a voice said from behind.

I turned to find Mrs. Hillingham with her hair teased and put up in a black scrunchie. She reminded me of Demi Moore in *St. Elmo's Fire*. Even dressed in an 80s costume, she looked gorgeous.

"Really? You had them made to look like Chanel purses?"

She shook her head. "No, these are actual Chanel purses from the 80s. You have no idea how much I paid my assistant to find them, but Seraphina had to have them for her party. And I love my daughter too much to tell her no for her birthday, especially her eighteenth birthday."

"Okay." I held back from telling her she should say no more often to that spoiled bitch, but who was I to tell her how to raise her daughter?

"Have you had a drink yet?" She placed her hand on my back, guiding me out of the hallway. We strolled into an enormous kitchen. The counters, floor, and waterfall island was marble, but all the cabinets were stainless steel.

It looked gorgeous and pristine. I worried about touching anything as the place was immaculate.

"No, I haven't. I'm not really . . ." My words died in my mouth when I moved closer and saw the display of food on the island. I had never seen so much food in one place. I thought Green Hills Academy's lunch was over the top, but Seraphina's party had it beat.

I had been so focused on the food that I hadn't noticed someone had walked in.

"Oh, Mrs. Hillingham. I didn't realize you were here." A woman with black hair pulled back in a bun and a crisp white button-up shirt and pants kept her gaze to the floor. She appeared nervous, and I wondered if I wasn't supposed to be in here.

"It's alright, Jane. A guest was looking for a drink." Crystal glanced around the room, apparently as lost as I was.

"Champagne or wine?" Jane looked at me, and I had never seen someone so void of feeling before. It was like she wasn't even human.

"Uh—"

"Champagne, Jane," Crystal answered for me. "It's a party, after all. Let's have some fun."

I stood there awkwardly as Jane uncorked a small bottle of champagne and stuck a straw in it. No glasses, I suppose. I never thought the rich would drink from the bottle.

"Aren't those adorable?" Crystal put her hand on my back again, guiding me out of the kitchen. "They're small enough that you can drink straight from the bottle. I went to a Gucci show last year, and they had them. I thought they were too cute."

Wow. This woman was way more cultured than I could ever hope to be.

"Most of the people are outside in the back." She pointed to a glass door.

Once we were outside, my breath caught. It was amazing. There was a pool and several small waterfalls pouring into it from over our heads on the second floor. And farther beyond were lounge chairs and a gazebo.

"Wow, your place is gorgeous."

"Thank you, Violet. Now let me see if I can find Seraphina for you." She glanced around, and I did too. Not that I wanted to find her but just to take in the scene.

I noticed a few celebrities swimming in the pool. It must have been heated because, being October, it wasn't warm out. Yet, somehow it felt warmer in the back than when I came to the party out front.

"Oh, there's Seraphina. I'll go grab her."

I watched Crystal walk around one waterfall and out toward the gazebo. Seraphina was standing there talking to a couple who looked like they stepped out of a magazine with their perfect skin, hair, and trendy bathing suits. I guess the 80s attire didn't apply to swimwear.

Once Crystal pointed in my direction, I could have sworn I saw Seraphina frown. But I blinked, and she had an enormous grin on her face and was waving at me.

Seraphina was gesturing me over when I heard something that stopped me in my tracks.

"You know she's using you," a female voice came from behind.

Harlow stood behind me in a bright pink bikini with a white sheer covering. She stepped closer to a heating lamp. Guess that explained why it was so warm out here.

"I figured. But why?"

Harlow's dark brown eyes slid to where Seraphina and her mom were standing. Neither of them were paying any attention to us. It looked as if they were in a serious discussion with a staff member.

"It's what Seraphina does. She takes on projects. But just know that there's always a reason. She never does it just for kicks. There's something about you that she wants," Harlow sneered, the words bitter on her tongue.

I hitched the Chanel bag on my shoulder. "It's not like I wanted any of this attention."

Her lips thinned. "Sure. That's why you're standing in Seraphina's backyard with her party bag on your shoulder."

"I get that you don't like me—"

"That's an understatement. But it's not because I'm jealous."

"I didn't think it was. I know I wasn't

born rich like you or Seraphina, but—"

Harlow threw her head back and laughed, cutting me off.

"You think I was born rich? I'll let you in on a little secret, sweetheart. I had to claw my way up the North Side ladder to get to where I am, and so did my parents. And from what I heard about Seraphina's mom, so did she. Did you know Mrs. Hillingham grew up in a trailer park on the South Side?"

My eyes widened. Maybe that was why Crystal was nicer to me than her daughter. Perhaps she felt some sort of kinship. She could relate to me based on our shared backgrounds.

"Really?" I turned my head and noticed Crystal was now over by the pool, pointing around the area with another worker at her side. "She acted so natural when I was shopping with her. It seemed like she'd had money all her life. Everything she did was effortless."

"Well, when you have dirt on everyone in town, you can act any way you want to."

A thought popped into my head. Was Crystal using me to find out more about Knight? She obviously couldn't get that information from her daughter—Knight hated Seraphina. I guessed she turned to me to get whatever she required.

"Does everyone use each other in this town?" I hadn't realized I said that out loud until Harlow answered me before heading over to the pool.

"How do you think we all have the money we do? Power isn't earned from good deeds. It's confiscated by the one left standing."

FOURTEEN

Violet

"GOING SO SOON? YOU'VE only been here an hour." Crystal came up behind me as I headed toward the kitchen.

Most of the people from the party were out on the back lawn watching the fireworks.

I shrugged. "It was fun, but I'm a little tired."

I wasn't tired, but I was incredibly bored. So much decadence was on display, from the food to the drinks to the ice sculptures that had vodka pouring out of them, and I wasn't impressed. Just because something cost a lot of money didn't mean it was quality.

The party was over the top. The only people I knew here were the ones I never wanted to hang out with in the first place.

She tilted her head. "I know you aren't tired. You're a teenager. I never heard of a teenager leaving at party at," she held up her wrist to check her watch, "nine o'clock because they were *tired.*"

I bit my bottom lip and glanced around. She caught me.

"Violet, I know you and my daughter didn't really get along before. And I'm not so naïve to believe that just because she acts nice to you and invites you to parties that you two will become best friends. But I had hoped you'd be a good influence on her."

"Me? Why me?"

She waved me through to the kitchen, and we sat at a round table near a picture window overlooking a large garden that flickered with the lights of the fireworks.

"I don't know if you know anything about me, but I'm from the South Side too."

"Actually, Harlow told me earlier . . .. But I have to say, it was a surprise. You seem so . . . elegant." I frowned at my embarrassing attempt at flattery.

It didn't matter because Crystal smiled and placed her hand on mine. "Thank you. I was young and caught the eye of a very handsome and very wealthy guy from the North Side."

She watched me for a moment. It felt like I was in a zoo and she was watching me, the wild animal, in my foreign enclosure.

"That's one reason I wanted my daughter to be friends with you. Maybe if I had some friends when I first stepped into this world, I wouldn't have felt so alone." Her gaze drifted off.

"I get that. It's like stepping onto an alien planet."

She squeezed my hand. "I may not be your mother, but you can come to me anytime, for anything. It must be rough not having her around."

"More than you know." My mind drifted to when I first moved into the pool house—that first night when I cried myself to sleep. I never told anyone about that. But that night I wished that when I woke up in the morning, I'd be back in the trailer and Mom would be there. That her death and North Green Hills had all been a terrible dream.

But when I woke up, I was in a room as big as the old trailer, and I knew it wasn't a dream.

My phone buzzed, and I lifted it from the bag I got for the party. It was Arabella texting me.

"My ride's here. Got to get going. Thank you for everything." I stood and moved toward the hallway, about to leave, but turned back. "You know, Seraphina is lucky to have a mom like you. I hope she knows that."

Crystal smiled. "Thank you, Violet. Here." She walked over and grabbed another party bag off the counter. They were scattered all over the house from guests who had put them down and walked away.

"Take another bag. Treat yourself." She winked.

I nodded. "Thanks again."

I turned and went through that door to the dark room and made my way out to the front of the house. An attendant opened Arabella's car door, and I slipped inside before he closed it.

"Oh my god, tell me everything! Who did you see there and what embarrassing stuff happened?"

I sighed and melted into the seat, happy to be driven away from that house.

"Here, you can have a party bag." I lifted it up, and she glanced over as she came to a stop at the end of the driveway.

"Holy motherfucking shit," she squealed and grabbed the purse from my hands, holding it up for inspection. "You got me one of the gift bags? Seraphina's party bags are like the Holy Grail of swag bags."

A horn blew behind us. "Why don't we look at them at home?"

"Yours or mine?" she asked while placing the purse in her lap and pulling out of the driveway.

Ugh, for a moment, I forgot about all the Knight drama.

"I guess head to Knight's place. I really

don't want to deal with him going all caveman and grilling me on where I've been and how the mayor could have hurt me. We can hang out in my room."

It didn't take long before we arrived in front of Knight's place because he lived on the same street. Arabella hugged the party bag to her chest as if it were a baby.

The house was quiet as we entered, but that was normal. It was so big that ten people could be here, and I wouldn't have a clue.

We got to my room, and as I opened the door, I saw movement beside my bed.

"What the— Ava?"

The little girl turned with wide gray eyes shining up at me. Her mouth formed an "O" of surprise.

"I did nothing," she said with darkening cheeks.

"If you didn't do anything," I smirked, "then why are you in my bedroom?"

Arabella and I walked farther into my

room.

"I was just, uh . . . making sure you had everything you needed." She jutted her chin forward, proud of her quick response.

"So, you weren't looking for this?" I held up my arm, my bracelet dangling from my wrist.

Arabella giggled. A few weeks ago, I told Ava that the bracelet was magical and made me a princess.

The little girl's eyes widened. She opened her mouth to speak but thought better of it and just shook her head.

"Well, if you aren't looking for my bracelet, then I'll just take it off and . . ." Ava didn't take her eyes off me as I removed my bracelet, "give it to Arabella."

Arabella held out her hand, and I plopped it into her palm. "Thank you, Violet. Looks like I have control now. So, what I want is, uh, huh . . . I don't know what I want you to do for me."

Ava was bouncing on her toes, and I could tell she desperately wanted to tell Arabella what to do, but she didn't have the bracelet.

"You know what? I'm hungry," Arabella announced.

"We have ice cream. Chocolate chip," Ava said with enthusiasm.

"Ice cream? Maybe . . . but wouldn't you rather have a bowl of Brussels sprouts or perhaps sardines?" Arabella tilted her head.

"Ew, yuck. No."

Arabella winked at me. "Okay, ice cream it is. Why don't we have an ice cream party?"

Ava jumped up and down, her little purple pajama dress fluttering around her calves. She darted past us and into the hallway. "Come on." We heard her yell from just outside the room. "My brother's asleep; he'll never know."

"She's adorable. To think she's related

to Knight," Arabella noted as we headed for the hallway.

"That was exactly my thought when I first met her."

Arabella had the Chanel purse hanging from her shoulder as we made our way downstairs and turned into the kitchen.

I looked up when I heard Knight.

"What are you doing out of bed?" he asked Ava.

She ignored him and reached into the freezer. "Getting ice cream. It's Saturday night, Dopey. Relax," she snapped back like a proper sister.

I snorted, and Arabella coughed out a laugh. Knight rolled his lips over his teeth, trying not to laugh too. Even the devil thought she was too cute for words.

"Just because it's Saturday doesn't mean you can stay up late. I'm in charge of you now and—"

"Then grab some bowls. They're too high for me to reach. And join the party,

Dopey. It's the weekend. That's when parties happen." She shook her hips, and both Arabella and I bent over in a fit of giggles.

"Yeah, Dopey," I said through my laughter.

"Hey, Ava. Why do you call your brother Dopey?" Arabella asked the question I never had to nerve to discover for myself.

Ava crawled up on the barstool on the far end of the kitchen island. "Because when I was young, he wore a hat that looked like Dopey from Snow White. I was really into Snow White at the time. Not the princess, but the queen from the movie."

"When you were young? As opposed to now, when you are . . ." Arabella raised her brow.

"Older. I mean, I'm not an old person like my brother, but I am more mature." She nodded as she grabbed a bowl from her brother and opened the container of chocolate chip ice cream.

My gaze slid over to Knight, and my breath hitched. His eyes locked onto mine. There was something there. Irritation, maybe?

It was when he turned to his sister and the intensity melted away—replaced by light and joy—that I realized how he felt about me.

Whatever attraction he had for me was gone. What was left behind was bitter disgust.

"I have to use the bathroom. I'll be right back," I said and dashed out of the room.

I ran to the hallway bathroom, shut the door, and locked it before I sank to the floor. Tears streamed down my face as the look on his face played over and over in my head.

I had known him less than two months, but in that time, he had taken hold of my thoughts—both good and bad. And while I hated to admit it, I liked the guy.

Maybe I was just one of those girls who couldn't get enough of the guy who was completely wrong for her. The bad boy—the one who would ultimately leave my heart in tatters.

That was when my confusion set in. I wanted to hate Knight. I wanted to tell him to fuck off, that I didn't need him, but that would be a lie.

I liked Knight, and that scared me.

I was frightened because I knew the loss of Knight's attention would create a crippling effect on my heart and leave me hollow.

FIFTEEN

Knight

SHE WAS RIGHT THERE, laughing, taunting me with her innocence.

For the first time since my parents died, I wanted to lose myself in the nothingness. Drift in a void free of thoughts and feelings.

Each night I got down on my knees and prayed that every emotion I had for Violet would be ground into dust and float away on the evening breeze.

"Damn, man, you look intense." Briggs slapped my back as he sat next to me at the lunch table.

Violet had moved back into my place this past weekend, and it was only Monday, and already, she had pissed me off. Telling me to leave after we fucked was bad, but I had told myself it was her way of dealing with living in the same house as me. That she needed time.

Then I discovered she went to Seraphina's birthday party. That was fucked-up. That bitch gave me Violet's tooth as a gift. And now they were friends?

My head filled with twisted thoughts that wouldn't go away.

"Violet moved back in on Friday," I

mumbled as my eyes slid to Briggs.

"What have I told you about spending too much time with girls? It fucks with your head." He tapped at the side of my head.

I rubbed my face and leaned back, staring at the wooden coffered ceiling. "I know. But it's my uncle . . .. She's not safe."

"From him or from you?"

Straightening, I shook my head. "My uncle, shithead."

Briggs chuckled. "Look, I know your uncle's up to something, but she's not your problem. As my mom would say, you're getting yourself twisted up like a pretzel over this girl."

"A girl twisted herself up like a pretzel? That I'd like to see," Caleb said as he pulled out his chair and sat on the other side of me.

"No, Knight's getting all twisted

because of some girl."

Caleb frowned. "Ugh, thanks for putting that mental image in my head, asshole."

I smirked. I could always count on these guys to put a smile on my face.

"I found out my uncle's been threatening Violet. He's been sending her cryptic notes. Obviously, he's trying to scare her."

Caleb tilted his head. "But why? From what you told us before, it seemed your uncle wanted her to stay. Why would he threaten her? Wouldn't that just scare her off and cause her to run away?"

Caleb was right. Why would my uncle want to keep her near him when he still lived in my house, but then try to scare her off with crazy notes?

"Oh, no. No, no, no." Briggs shook his head.

"What?" I asked.

"That look." He pointed at me. "I know that look. You want to do even more digging. Find out why he sent those notes."

I had been pondering it ever since I discovered that the paper stock matched.

Our servers came over and placed food trays in front of us. I had a burger, while both Briggs and Caleb had steak.

Briggs picked up his fork and knife and dug in, while Caleb and I pushed our trays away. I wasn't hungry. It seemed the roller-coaster ride of feelings I had for Violet caused me to lose my appetite. I had no idea why Caleb wasn't eating.

"And what if I do? Why do you care?"

Briggs' lips thinned. "Because it always ends up with some crazy shit going down. Like when you found Violet at Happy Pond back in the spring. Or that body showing up in the basement."

"Like I made all that happen." I rolled my eyes and threw my hands up in frustration. "I'm not the fucked-up one here. That's my uncle. Someone lured Violet's mom to the pond . . .."

A thought popped into my head as I was defending myself. *Violet's mom.* Why was she there that night?

I had expected my uncle to show up. That was why I was there, to catch him in some shady act or, at the very least, overhear him talk about his plan.

But he wasn't there. There was some guy I couldn't make out and then Violet's mom. It looked like she gave him a plastic bag filled with something.

I never found out what it was before I stupidly stepped on a stick that snapped, causing them to look my way. I hid for several minutes, and when I knew the coast was clear, I went back to find the guy walking up from the pond without Violet's mom.

I had assumed she left. When I leaned closer, I must have disturbed a bird because it flew out of the woods. The guy was doing something by a canoe near the edge of the pond but ran when he heard the bird. That was when I went to investigate and found Violet's mom in the canoe.

"So what if Violet's mom was there to buy drugs? Again, this isn't your problem. I am only saying this to you as a friend. That girl is bad news." Briggs placed his hand on my shoulder.

My gaze shifted to Violet. She rolled her eyes at something Seraphina had said. I chuckled, watching her. I liked her tough spirit.

"I don't think she is. I think she's caught in a messed-up game of power and money." I turned to Briggs. "I think that girl is the key to some golden chest my uncle desperately wants to open."

Briggs was silent for a moment before he let out a deep sigh. "I love you, man. You're like a brother to me. And if finding out if something shady went on with her mom's death is what you want to do, I'll help you. But just know, I can't get in trouble this year. I got into Winter Rivers University for football, and they can take that offer back at any time."

I understood how important it was for Briggs to get picked for one of the best college football teams in the country. Winter Rivers might not have been in the top five, but it was usually in the top ten, and professional football teams always recruited from there.

"I've kept you guys in the dark as much as possible. I promise not to ask for anything that might get you in trouble."

"Feel free to get me in trouble as much as you want, Knight," Caleb said as he slid his hands behind his head.

"Noted. What I'm curious about is Seraphina's sudden interest in Violet."

"Yeah, that's completely suspect." Briggs raised a brow.

"It was her dad's bus company that Violet was trapped in. She's doing it to make daddy happy. So Violet doesn't consider suing."

"That makes sense, but I don't think that's everything. I mean, Violet hasn't acted like she was going to sue. And even if she did, I know Mr. Hillingham did an internal investigation and already paid for her hospital bills." I rubbed my chin.

"Still. She could sue anyway. And she'd have a pretty excellent case since Seraphina locked her on the bus," Caleb pointed out.

"There's something else I found out. But it has to do with Seraphina's mom."

The guys leaned in as Briggs pushed his empty tray back.

"I got some information about a failed cancer drug that Jack Franklin had been working on in Franklin Laboratories before he died. Apparently, my uncle invested in it, as did Kiki and one other person."

Caleb waved his hand for me to continue.

"It was Mrs. Hillingham. She invested a lot of money into the drug."

Caleb shrugged. "So? It could have cured cancer. I would have invested in it if Jack came to me before he died. Not that he would have, since I was only sixteen, but you get my point."

"No." I shook my head. "It failed phase

one of testing. Then Jack died. And that's when they all invested. After the failure and after he died. Why would they do that?"

Both of the guys looked confused.

"Let me get this straight. They put up a lot of money in a failed drug and after the head of the company was no more? That is shady," Briggs said exactly what I was thinking.

We were all silent for a moment. Briggs helped himself to a few fries from my plate. The guy constantly ate.

"What if they're still working on the drug?" Caleb asked with a look of revelation. He sat up and turned to face me. "What if they wanted to use that drug for something else? Something that would make them a bunch of money."

"Oh my god, that makes total sense," I commented and wanted to kick myself for not thinking about it before.

Now I had to find out what became of that drug. But that still didn't answer why Seraphina was friends with Violet and why Violet was hanging with her willingly.

SIXTEEN

Violet

"ISN'T THIS FUN? IT'S even raining, just like the movies. It was a dark and stormy night . . ." Arabella said as she pulled into the school parking lot.

"Yeah, a blast," Jewel commented from the backseat and shook her head. "And it's not raining anymore."

It was Tuesday night, and we were here to let Jewel into the school. Only Arabella's headlights lit up the school parking lot as we pulled in.

"Well, you might be used to more thrilling evenings, but the last time we came here in the dark, we found a giant hole that apparently had a dead body in it. Though, we didn't know it at the time." Arabella put the car into park.

I glanced around the parking lot. "Are there people still here?" I pointed at a car parked in front of the school.

Arabella frowned. "I guess it's a janitor. But this place is so big, I doubt you'll run into him."

"No biggie if I do. I'll just pretend I'm a new maintenance person. This isn't the first time I was in a building I wasn't supposed to be in." Jewel winked.

We hopped out of the car and made our way to the side of the building.

"Just know that all the doors inside will be locked. I have a spare key that will get you into the gym locker rooms and the art room, but I couldn't get a hold of more." Arabella rolled her eyes. "My dad caught me. I had to make up some bullshit about learning how to make a key in shop."

"You take shop?" I asked in surprise.

"Of course. You never know when metalwork will come in handy." Arabella shrugged.

I elbowed her. "But you can't actually make keys."

"I never said that." She fluttered her fingers in the air. "These have magical powers."

Damn, what couldn't that girl do? She knew about the hole in the basement, everyone's secret past, and made keys from scratch.

"Shit. Why am I bothering with you, Violet? I should have been making nice with Red over here." Jewel threw her thumb over her shoulder at Arabella.

"The point of this is, I need these back. So just leave them under the second bush along the wall." Arabella pointed to a row of tall green bushes that lined the wall of the building.

"I'll unlock the main door to the school, and once you're in, the door will lock behind you. You'll be able to get out, but not back inside. This key," she pulled the key out of her black leather jacket pocket and placed it in Jewel's hand, "will get you inside the rooms I told you about."

Jewel nodded. "Thanks."

She moved toward the door. I went to get back into Arabella's car when I heard a door open. It wasn't the door Jewel was opening—it was much louder and heavier, and made a creaking noise.

"I think it's coming from the front," Arabella said as she came up behind me.

I nodded. She had heard it too.

Instead of hopping in the car, we walked around the building toward the front.

"The only person in the building should be the janitor. And I know it takes the janitor longer to clean the place. My dad said he's there most nights until three in the morning."

"He wasn't there the night we broke in and found the hole."

"That was a Saturday night." Arabella gave me a lopsided smile. "Even janitors need days off, Violet."

"Right." I felt stupid for not putting that together.

We peeked around the corner of the

brick building. Someone was heading toward that car we saw in the front parking lot when we arrived.

"Is that—" I mumbled before my voice died in my throat.

"I think it is. And that plastic covering sure looks like it's covered in blood," Arabella whispered.

My heart pounded in my chest. Was there going to be another dead body in that hole come morning?

"Holy fuck," I gasped as she started the car and the headlight shone right on us.

We both took a quick step back, and I closed my eyes tight, hoping we had not been seen.

"This is so fucked-up. Shit. Did she see us?" Arabella muttered.

I wanted to answer her, but that was when I heard someone call out my name.

"Violet? Violet, is that you?" she asked,

and the last thing I wanted to do was answer.

But I had to decide as I heard the footsteps grow closer. She had turned the car off and was walking toward us, but the headlights were still focused in our direction.

I had to decide between running like a coward and hope she wouldn't catch us—which I knew she would—or step out and sacrifice myself with the anticipation that she hadn't seen Arabella.

I took a deep breath and placed my hand on Arabella's shoulder, jerking my head for her to get away.

With eyes filled with dread, she shook her head. Her hands clasped, basically pleading with me not to go. My mother and, to an extent, my aunt hadn't raised a coward.

I took a step and rounded the corner,

the bright beam of light blinding me.

"I thought I saw you. What are you doing here so late at night? And on a Tuesday?" Mrs. Hillingham asked as she stopped in front of me.

She was a dark figure. She was so close, yet I couldn't tell what she was wearing as the light created a bright halo that surrounded her but darkened her body.

I was glad I couldn't see the blood on her coat. That image would never leave my mind.

"I could have sworn my bracelet dropped in the field during gym. I was looking for it." I held my breath, hoping she had believed me.

"At night?"

A nervous laugh bubbled out of my mouth. *Shit.* It was a ridiculous lie.

Crystal took a step closer, and my heart raced. Was she about to grab me and toss me into her trunk? Or worse, throw me down that hole?

Her hand rested on my shoulder, and I froze. I braced myself in case I had to run.

"Look, Violet, I understand if you don't want to tell me why you're really here. I was your age once too. Hanging out on the school field with a boy or to party with my friends. I get it. But just be safe, okay?"

I nodded and let out a breath filled with relief.

"Since your mom isn't around anymore, let me give you some advice."

"Okay." I bit my lip, wishing our talk would end so I could go home and hide under my bed.

"It's about Knight . . .. That boy has been through a lot. While it's not my place to tell you what to do, I don't think you should let him do anything you aren't comfortable with. I'm not saying that because he broke up with Seraphina. If anything, I'm glad that happened."

She shook her head. "I'm saying that because I've seen how he's changed since his parents' tragic death. And he hasn't changed for the better. He refuses to move on. He kept telling Seraphina the crash wasn't an accident. And, well, it makes me sad to think he's created this villain in his head who wanted his parents dead."

My eyes widened. Did she know Knight suspected his uncle?

"Did you know that when it first happened, he blamed my husband?"

No, I hadn't known.

"Why would he think your husband had anything to do with it?"

"Because it was a Hillingham plane. Our business is in transportation, though our bus line is the biggest part of the company, but we also have a few small commercial planes and trains."

I gasped. No wonder Knight blamed Seraphina's dad. His parents died on Mr. Hillingham's plane.

"I just think that boy looks for trouble. And if you look hard enough, you are bound to find something. Whether it's true or not makes no difference to him."

What she said made sense. Knight always had an air about him—bitter and on edge. As much as I was considering what she told me, it didn't negate the fact that she walked out of the school with what looked like a rain slicker covered in blood.

She removed her hand, and her eyes widened. "Oh, no."

I glanced over to my shoulder. She had left a bloody handprint behind. My stomach flip-flopped, and I hoped I wouldn't puke.

"Oh, god." I winced.

"I'm so sorry, Violet."

I glanced back as fear crept up my neck. There was no way she was letting me go now, not with evidence on my sweater—her handprint.

I stared at her with round eyes as my mind thought up ways to escape. Would Jewel hear me if I screamed?

The school walls were thick, and I doubted she would hear an explosion, let alone a teenage girl being murdered in a parking lot.

"The icing got everywhere, and I was in such a rush, I didn't wipe my hands properly. I hope it doesn't stain."

"Icing?"

She groaned, but a smile appeared on her face. "It was supposed to be a surprise. I have a Pumpkin Luncheon every year for charity. It's a big thing, and I personally invite people with small gift baskets.

Sometimes I do pumpkin cookie baskets, and one year I did a pumpkin bread basket. This year I went with pumpkin cupcakes decorated with red icing. Big mistake. Several of the cupcakes, well . . . they got all over me. Thankfully, I was wearing my rain slicker."

I heard Arabella from around the corner as she whispered, "Oh."

Crystal glanced back at her car, but she must have thought that was me. "The principal lets me sneak in during the night and leave the baskets on people's desks and in lockers. And since I've already ruined the surprise, there's one for you too."

My eyebrows shot up. "Oh, that's so nice. Thank you."

My grin was large, and it wasn't from being invited to her luncheon. It was utter relief that I wouldn't be murdered tonight.

"I should get back. Do you need a ride, Violet?"

"No, I'm okay. I, uh . . . got to borrow a friend's car."

She nodded and winked. "Whatever you say. Enjoy the cupcakes."

With that, she waved and headed back to her car. I watched as she hopped in and drove off, then I fell back against the brick wall and slid to the ground.

Someone came out of the shadows and stood over me.

"That was the scariest ten minutes of my life. I wouldn't be surprised if I went home and looked in the mirror and found some gray hair," Arabella said as she stood over me.

"Yes. I really believed she was going to kill me." I burst into laughter.

Arabella joined in and sat beside me. We both let out the tension as we chuckled.

"What I don't get is why she was delivering them to the school?" Arabella asked as we finally got up and headed back to her car.

"She said she likes to hand-deliver them."

"No, she doesn't." Arabella slid into the driver's seat as I got in the passenger side. "I know lots of people who get invited, and not once did Crystal deliver the invite herself. She's wealthy; she hires people to do that for her."

"She wasn't always rich, you know."

"Really?" Arabella's head tilted toward me right after she turned on the car.

"You didn't know that? But you know everything."

"I do, which is weird that I didn't know that. And now that I think about it, I don't know much of anything about Seraphina's mom. Huh." Arabella rubbed her chin. "Looks like I'm going to do some digging."

That was strange that Arabella didn't know about Crystal's past. Was it some closely guarded secret? And if so, why?

SEVENTEEN

Violet

"**What are you doing** in here?" I stared at my bed from my bedroom doorway in Knight's home.

I had arrived home from school, happy it was Friday and the week was over. Knight had avoided me most of the week until now.

"Our art project is due in a few weeks. We need to get started." His gray eyes lingered on me.

He sat back, propping himself up on his elbows. The guy looked like he needed his fitted dark, faded jeans and black T-shirt ripped from his body. And my mouth watered as I imagined tearing his clothes off with my teeth.

A sigh escaped my lips, but I kept my eyes to the floor, refusing to let him enjoy the desire that burned inside me.

"I guess you want to do the project in my bed?"

That came out wrong. I grimaced as he chuckled.

"I would totally be up for that."

The ache in my head throbbed from waking from a nightmare last night. I dreamed about the pond, the night my mom died. But in this dream, I was standing next to her. She kept saying, "She deserves it all," to a mysterious person in a hoodie. Try as I might, I couldn't see the person's face.

She reached out and grabbed her arm, dragging her into the pond while I stood there, unable to move, watching in alarm as she drowned. I screamed, but it didn't help. That was when I woke, sweat causing the T-shirt I slept in to stick to my body.

But last night was a different type of fear. As I threw my backpack onto the floor by my desk and strolled into the room, the anxiety I felt was directed at Knight. I worried how my body would react to his touch. Would I melt into his grip like always?

There was no way I was going near my bed.

Occasionally fucking was one thing, but something happened the last time. I saw it in his eyes. He wanted more with me, or maybe he wanted more control over me.

And when he took whatever he gave me away, it felt as if my heart split in two.

If what Crystal said on Tuesday was true, it was best we stayed housemates and nothing more.

I sat on the chair by my desk and watched Knight. He lay back, intertwining his fingers behind his head, staring at the ceiling.

"I'm not the devil. You know that, right? It's a stupid nickname someone gave me, and it stuck. But that's not who I am."

He wasn't even looking at me, his gaze locked on the fan spinning over my bed.

"Why would someone give you that nickname if it's not like you?"

Maybe he refused to accept what others saw in him.

He rubbed his face and sat up. "Because I ruin people. To them, I'm the devil because if anyone crossed me, I made damn sure they never did it again."

My mouth fell open. I knew he was bad, but I had never heard about any of that.

His fingers pulled through his hair as his lips tightened. "I was angry when my parents died. And that's how I reacted to the world. If someone even shifted their line of sight in my direction, I vowed to destroy them. I'm a twisted little fuck." Knight laughed, but it was as sharp as his words.

"You were grieving. Grief makes us think and do crazy things," I said, remembering my experiences when my mom died.

Like the time my aunt got a call from my principal about the fight I started. It wasn't right what I did, but I had tremendous anger running through my veins. I thought I would explode unless I let it out.

But I paid the price. That was why my aunt so easily accepted the mayor's offer for me to go live with him for my senior year. I had been a little devil too—too much to handle for a relative who was barely around.

"But that's the thing, Violet; I'm still that twisted little menace." He pointed at the side of his head as he scooted off the bed. "I'm still angry every day. I think about what I would do if my uncle was alone in a room with me. Every. Single. Day."

I stood and walked over to him. "And I don't? Maybe he took your parents from you, but he tried to take my soul."

My fingernails dug into the palm of my hand just remembering that day. When he held me down on the pool house floor and dug his fingers into my thighs. I was angry too.

Knight caressed my head, kissing the top. "He's going to pay for what he did, Violet."

"Like Mr. Hillingham?" I blurted out.

I didn't understand why I said that. Maybe I believed Seraphina's mom and wanted to know if the anger Knight felt for his uncle was justified.

Ichabod King might have been a rapist, but that didn't mean he was a murderer.

Knight stiffened and stepped back. "What?"

"When your parents first died, you blamed Seraphina's dad."

His jaw ticked. "I guess Seraphina told you."

I wasn't about to correct him. It didn't matter where I heard it from. Based on his reaction, I knew it was true. Mrs. Hillingham hadn't lied when she told me that.

"Just because they were in one of his planes doesn't mean Mr. Hillingham was trying to kill them."

He nodded. "I guess she didn't mention that Jack Franklin bought the plane earlier that week from Mr.

Hillingham. While I don't know if he had anything to do with the plane going down, I know the problem with the plane was caused by faulty maintenance. Something a plane technician would have easily caught."

"Did they charge Jack's plane tech?"

He shook his head. "The police can't charge a dead man."

I gasped, "What the fuck?"

"Now do you see why I am looking for answers? They know, Violet. My uncle, probably Kiki, and some others I am just figuring out . . . they know the plane was rigged to crash, and they've been keeping it a secret."

For the first time, I understood. I knew why Knight was so angry. Why he was locked away. And that made me upset too.

I stepped forward and lifted my arms, clasping my fingers behind his neck. "I'm sorry," I whispered as our foreheads touched.

"I'm sorry too. I never kept this from you because I didn't trust you. I kept it from you to protect you. There are many people in this town who only care about money and power. They don't care if someone gets hurt. They don't care that they took my parents away. And I know they don't care that your mom died, either. Anything can be made to look like an accident or an overdose. This town is filled with liars, cheats, thieves, and murderers . . . and I'm not talking about the South Side."

"I thought coming up here, living in this grand home and going to such a prestigious school would be amazing. I never thought my life would be worse off living up here."

"What they've done to us is fucked-up, but I promise I'll make them pay."

Knight's mouth crashed onto mine. The rage that had built up for the past two years tugged at my lips. He bit me, and his fingers clawed at my clothes until they were a pile on the ground.

When I stepped back, he pushed me onto the bed. My back hit the bed, and my dark hair fanned out on the creamy silk bedspread.

It wasn't long before he was naked and rolling on a condom from his pocket. He stepped forward, crawled onto the bed, and hovered over me.

There was no foreplay, no caresses, not even a dirty phrase. This was just fucking. That was what he wanted. And he had been through too much for me not to spread my legs and help ease his pain.

Knight stared at me with searching gray eyes. As his cock slid inside and my eyes glazed over from the feel of him, Knight watched me like a lion observing his prey.

He rocked into me, and heat slid up from my core. I wrapped my arms around him, clinging, wanting more. He knew it too.

But he never gave it to me. Was that the twisted Knight he had told me about? Taunting me until I writhed around and begged for more.

"Please," I said with a grunt.

He reached over and pinned my hands back. "No."

I gnashed my teeth. The asshole knew what he was doing. Now I couldn't relieve the pressure building in my clit.

"You're an asshole." My voice was a hoarse whisper.

That got him to stop staring at me. He lowered his head, his hot breath snaking down my sweat-slicked neck.

"You knew what I was when you first opened your pussy for me. And you're still doing it."

Those words. I should hate him, but my body didn't. I arched my back, reaching for anything he'd throw my way.

"Why do you let me fuck you?" Knight

tightened his grip on my wrists, his hips jerking in and out at an irritatingly steady pace.

I shook my head frantically. "I don't know."

He was awful. Getting in bed with him was the worst mistake of my life, but it was also the most thrilling ride I had ever experienced, one I never wanted to end.

"I do. I know why your panties get soaked when I come near."

"Don't fucking flatter yourself," I said as I wrapped my legs around him, pulling him closer.

"Because I give you what you want. I do all the things you love to your body, even the things you never told anyone. You know deep down there's no one who can make you come like me."

I was about to make another smartass comment when he sat up. He pulled me with him, so I was seated on his lap.

"Hold on while I make you come," the

confident fuck said with a smirk.

But as his hand drifted over my ass cheek, I felt his finger slip over my puckered hole. My head fell back at the thrill of what he was about to gift me.

He was right. Knight knew what I liked.

His finger slid around and around, teasing me.

I whimpered and lifted my head, begging him with my stare. He was watching me again, but this time, his eyes were as needy as mine. It was in that moment I realized the twisted devil's little secret.

He got off on my need. Knight wanted me to beg for him. He had a fucked-up superhero complex that only he could satisfy me. Not that I thought no one else could make me come like he could; it was that he needed me to believe that.

"Please, Knight. Fill me. Make me come."

It was what he wanted to hear, and

deep down, I wanted to make the fucker happy.

His nose flared, and within seconds, his finger slid in and out of my asshole, working in tandem as heat coiled in my core.

I was tightening around his cock as I shifted my hips up and down.

"Fuck," I ground out as my climax ripped through my body. The world darkened around me as I rode out my orgasm.

"Yes, Violet." Knight's hand pushed me down on his cock, shifting his hip, riding his own wave.

We both stopped pushing, stopped taking. We held each other with only our chests rising and falling, the sounds of our breath like whispers of reality settling on our shoulders.

He shifted, and I knew it was time to move away. It was time to slip off him and make an awkward excuse as to why he should leave.

I pushed myself off his lap. Knight looked over at me, his finger lifting to trace my chin. I felt a shiver, and I hated that when the beauty between us faded, we turned into enemies again.

We danced the tightrope between love and hate, and I feared it would break. Which side would we fall on?

"I guess we got a little distracted and didn't work on our project." He gave me a half smile.

"Seems like it."

"How about we order pizza and work on it tonight? Unless, uh . . . you have other plans." His eyes darted to the side.

Wait. Was he nervous? He rubbed the back of his neck. And that awkward stutter in the question he asked.

I blinked in surprise before a smile broke out on my face. This was a side of Knight I had never seen. A cute boy wanting to spend time with a girl.

"I don't have plans," I said and took a breath, trying to settle my wildly beating heart.

EIGHTEEN

Violet

"**HOLY SHIT, DID YOU** hear that Seraphina hooked up with Delano Rogers at her birthday party? Look." Arabella shoved her phone in my face.

I set down my latte and plucked the phone from her fingers.

"Oh yeah. I remember seeing him there. He was dressed up like Jason Patric from *The Lost Boys*. Man, he's hot. I don't blame her at all."

It was Sunday afternoon, and Arabella and I were waiting on Jewel at The Drip. I had spent most of the weekend with Knight.

Things between us became a little less confusing after we fucked on Friday and worked on our project. We were acting like a genuine couple.

I swear I couldn't stop smiling whenever I thought about him. When I brought him up after Arabella and I first arrived at the coffee shop, she told me I was officially annoying. That all couples hit an annoying stage, and I had it bad.

"I'm pretty sure her mom's not too happy. Apparently, he's not known for being a one girl sort of guy."

I shrugged. "We're in high school. It's not like Seraphina is going to marry the guy."

Arabella tilted her head. "Do you know nothing about Delano?"

I shook my head. I wasn't about to tell her I didn't realize he was famous. The only reason I noticed him at the party was because he was good-looking, nothing else.

"He's in all the teen musical movies."

I nodded. That was why I didn't recognize him. I wasn't a musical sort of person.

"Thanks for meeting me." Jewel appeared at the table and startled me. I hadn't realized she came into the coffee shop.

She slid in a chair next to me, and her eyes darted around the room.

"I found the key," Arabella said.

"Yeah, that's not why I asked you meet me here."

"Okay. Then what is it? Is everything okay?" I asked, a little worried.

If someone like Jewel was nervous, then it had to be bad.

"It's my cousin. I gave you his phone."

"The one who drove the bus," I added with a nod.

"He's missing. Like, straight-up gone. No one can find him. I've called him. Gone to all his usual places. Nothing."

Arabella gave me a look, and it wasn't good.

"For how long?"

"At least a week. I texted him the day after you let me inside the school, and he never got back. The last time I saw him before that was the previous Sunday. I'm worried about him. That stupid idiot got himself into some shit. I know it has to do with that bus accident. Like I told you before, he's been going straight for a while. There's no way he owes anyone."

I bit my bottom lip. That was strange.

"Maybe he went on vacation? Took his new car on the road." I tried to come up with something to help her feel better.

She grabbed a sugar packet and made tiny tears along the edge. "No. The car is still in his parking spot. It's like he took a walk and never came back."

"Holy shit," Arabella let out and leaned back in her chair.

"The phone. Have you found anything on it?" she asked with hope in her eyes.

I shook my head. "No, but I gave it to a..." I hesitated, not sure what to call Knight. We weren't boyfriend and girlfriend. At least, I didn't think we were. "To a friend. He's the one who has all the shit on people. If anyone can find anything, he can."

"I hope you're right."

"Did you get done what you needed to do at the school on Tuesday?" I asked, trying to change the subject.

Maybe if we talked about something else, it would help her relax.

"Not really. I tried going in the locker room, but it was blocked. There was something on the other side of the door, but I couldn't tell what it was. It doesn't matter. I'm not doing that shit anymore, not after what has happened to my cousin. I'm done with this town. There's a furniture manufacturer upstate that's hiring. I'm taking my kid and going there."

I frowned but reached over and placed my hand on hers. "I understand. Look, if my boyfriend finds anything, I'll let you know. Okay?"

She nodded. "I got to go. There's a lot

of packing to do, and I need to pick up my kid from my neighbor's apartment."

"Okay. Good luck," Arabella said as Jewel got up.

I watched her as she left.

"That's crazy, Violet. First, that guy who almost raped you got killed, and then the guy driving the bus where you were stuck inside goes missing. Both of these men were involved in harming you."

"I don't really think Jewel's cousin was trying to hurt me. I don't think he knew what was going to happen."

Arabella reached for my hand, her expression pained. "I know you're in love, but—"

"I'm not in love." I rolled my eyes. "I like Knight. I like him a lot. Sure, he's a little fucked-up, but he's been through some shit. And I think he really wants to protect me."

Her lips thinned. "That's exactly my worry. He wants to protect you. But what's his idea of protecting? Going after the people who hurt you?"

I picked at the brown paper protector that hugged the middle of the coffee cup. Would Knight go that far?

"Think about it, Violet. He had the guy's phone. I'm sure there was something on it that showed where he could be found. An address to his home or work. Something. He could have tracked down Jewel's cousin and made him disappear."

"What about John Lenker? Why would he bail me out if he killed the guy? Wouldn't Knight want to frame someone else?"

"Yes, someone else, but not you. Didn't Seraphina say that the cops told her some recent evidence came up right after you were bailed out of jail? That's a little too much of a coincidence for me."

Heat traveled up my neck. I glanced around the shop. There were some couples sharing laughs and one kissing. That was what I wanted—something normal and sweet.

But Knight wasn't that—he was dark and twisted; he was the devil. His touch branded me while his words burned as I spoke them. Because deep down, I knew he was the devil.

"That's exactly what it is, Arabella. A coincidence. Knight's not the bad guy."

I couldn't even look at her as I said it because deep down, I knew he *was* the devil.

NINETEEN

Knight

I STROLLED INTO ART class Monday morning with the biggest grin on my face. There were dark clouds looming through the windows, and I knew any minute a storm would break, but I didn't care.

It was the first time in two years that I

was happy. Being with Violet this weekend felt wonderful. We joked, got takeout, played with Ava, and then at night, we fucked our brains out.

She seemed a bit off on Sunday evening, but I suspected she was tired from me waking her early by going down on her.

"Did you break your face?" Caleb asked as he pointed at me.

I slid into my seat at our usual art table. "No."

"A new haircut?" Briggs side-eyed me.

I shook my head. "Nope."

"Wait, I know what it is. You finally lost your virginity to that cousin you always had a crush on," Caleb commented with a chuckle.

"Fuck you." I laughed along with him.

"What the hell? Why all smiles?"

Right at that moment, Violet walked into the room. I locked my eyes on her, and she did the same.

"Oh, no. Please tell me this isn't so," Briggs said.

"Knight is actually in love. I never thought I'd see the day," Caleb said, straightening in his seat.

"I'm not in love. We're just fucking. What can I say? She's a good lay." I tried my best to throw them off, but I was wondering about my feelings too.

Was I in love with Violet?

But the closer she moved to the table, the faster my heart beat in my chest. When I woke this morning, it was the first time in two years I hadn't thought of my parents' death.

Every morning for the past two years, I woke up angry, sometimes depressed. But today I felt alive and happy to be so.

"You're in a good mood. Did Ms. Chiron give us all As without having to turn in our projects?" Violet asked as she sat.

A whiff of vanilla filled the air, and I

leaned closer.

“She’ll give us As anyway. I have never heard of a kid failing her class. She doesn’t want to deal with our parents,” Briggs said.

“Really? So, we don’t even have to work on the art project?”

Caleb shrugged. “Just turn in a can of soup and say Warhol inspired you. It’s that easy.”

I gazed over at them. “Now I know what you two are doing for your project.”

“I thought it was clever,” Briggs added. “But then again, I’m not an artist.”

We all chuckled. I heard my phone buzz in my backpack and reached in to grab it. It was a message from Edwin.

He had called me earlier, but I missed it. My eyes grew wide as I read the message.

“What’s wrong?” Briggs asked.

“It’s Edwin, my uncle’s assistant. He’s been arrested.”

“What?” Violet reached over and

placed her hand on my arm.

"He's been helping me get information from my uncle . . . along with other tasks."

I didn't want them to know everything. There were some things Edwin did that might not be seen as helpful, especially to Violet.

Especially considering what had happened with her mom.

Briggs leaned in and lowered his voice. "Did your uncle find out?"

"He must have. Because Edwin's being arrested for John Lenker's murder." I rubbed my brow and reread the message.

Caleb shook his head. "Shit. Do you think he did it?"

"No, I don't think he did it," I snapped. "It's obvious my uncle is trying to pin it on him."

Caleb sat back and held up his hand. "I was just asking. You know the guy, not me."

"Look, I'm sorry. It's just . . . I'm pissed.

And worried. I have come so far and now this." I waved at my phone.

Violet's brow wrinkled. "You've come far? What about him? I can't imagine he's happy to be arrested for something he didn't commit."

I angled my head and stared at her. What the fuck was her problem?

"I'm sure he's not, especially since he has a family. But that's the thing. I don't. The only family I have left is a little girl who depends on me. He has a wife who can help him. Who do I have?"

Her head jerked back. "Wow, Knight . . . Just wow." Violet stood and reached for her backpack.

I grabbed her arm before she could lift it. "Where are you going? Class isn't over."

"Away from you. You just told me that man is innocent, yet all you can whine about is how this hurts you. Not him. Not how it devastates his wife and kids. Just you. I thought you were different than these spoiled assholes, but you're just like them. It's always how it negatively affects you."

She jerked her hand away, hooking her backpack on her shoulder, and I watched her walk up to the teacher. They discussed something before Ms. Chiron nodded and pointed to the door. Violet never looked back as she strolled right out of class.

"Damn, that was harsh." Caleb had a habit of telling others his opinion, even when it wasn't warranted.

"She's not wrong, though," Briggs said.

I turned my gaze to him, narrowing my eyes. "You agree with her? That's a first." I clenched my fist, wanting to hit something. If Briggs kept it up, it might be him.

"Yes, I agree. You say this dude's been helping you and not one mention of how you plan to help him out. Just complaining about how it affects you. Sounds like something your uncle would say." Briggs' eyes focused on me, refusing to budge.

My jaw clenched.

"When Violet was arrested, you did the same thing. I said nothing then because I didn't like her. But her sticking up for him just now, a man she doesn't even know . . . that girl cares about people. I was wrong about her. I thought she was just using you, but someone like that doesn't use people. They get used."

I wasn't an idiot. I knew what Briggs was insinuating.

"You think I'm using her? I bailed her out of jail." I threw my hands up because what the fuck? How had I suddenly turned into the bad guy in my friend's eyes?

"I'm your friend. That will not change. But the game you're playing is risky and dangerous. You pull people in, and then when they get fucked, you shrug like they should just take it. All the time only concerned how it will be a problem for you."

Silence fell onto the table. Briggs and I stared at each other, daring each other to look away. As for Caleb, I suspected he didn't want to get into the middle of our mess.

But as I sat there, Briggs' words sank in. I had focused my mind on discovering the truth about my parents for so long that everything related to it was an afterthought. My association with Edwin and even my relationship with Violet were tied to my uncle.

I frowned. My life had been a lie. Every decision I made was to get my uncle.

I shook off the guilt. There was a reason I had to focus on my uncle. That reason was bigger than worrying about my friends. There was a monster out there, and he needed to be brought down.

I wished I could explain it all to them. Maybe if I did, they would understand. But if I did that, they'd be in more danger.

One day, when it all ended and my

uncle was behind bars, I had a feeling they wouldn't want to be around me anymore.

"I can't be seen helping him. That's what my uncle wants. Edwin knew the risks when he agreed to help." I shrugged. "The most I can do is pay for his bail, like I did for Violet. After that, he's on his own."

But he'd be a dead man walking, and that made me uneasy.

The bell rang, and Briggs' expression grew dark. He stood, never taking his eyes off me.

"I never believed it when people called you The Devil. But now I understand," he said and turned, mixing in with the kids as he walked out of class.

I sat there while the class emptied—even Caleb left without a word. I was alone and worried that if I continued down the path I set for myself, there wouldn't be anyone I loved left.

TWENTY

Violet

MY EYES BLINKED OPEN from another night of troubled sleep. I reached for my phone to check the time—three in the morning.

"You're awake." A deep voice in the darkness startled me.

Gasping, I sat up and scanned my room. A dark figure was seated at my desk, watching me.

"Knight?" I squeaked and cleared my throat.

"You were crying."

After wiping my cheek, I rubbed my fingers together. They were wet. Tears.

"You came in to check on me?"

"I've been here a while. Thinking. Then you began to cry."

I pulled the covers close to my chest as a shiver ran through me. Knight had been in my room watching me as I slept.

"What the fuck? You know how creepy you sound right now, right?"

He ran his fingers through his hair and groaned. "Right. I know." He jumped up with an unusual amount of pep for how early it was in the morning. "I didn't want to be alone. I didn't want you to . . . Fuck."

He walked over to the curtains. The moon was full and let in a faint light that made him glow as if he were some otherworldly creature who only came out at night.

I pulled the covers back and slid out of bed. The floor was cool on my feet as I stepped toward Knight.

"This week has been tough on me too. I hate not trusting you, Knight. But just when I think you're a good guy, that you care about me, you do something that's totally fucked-up. How you acted with your friend who got arrested . . . is that how you acted when I was locked up?"

He swiveled toward me and grabbed my arms. I hadn't noticed, but he had dark circles under his eyes.

I had avoided him all week at school and stayed at Arabella's until late in the evening, only coming back here to sleep.

His excuse for the arrest was awful. And it made me wonder if I really knew anything about Knight. Maybe he tried to kill his uncle when he was sixteen. Maybe

Seraphina, while vapid, wasn't the monster he made her out to be.

"No, it's not." He sighed and let his hands fall to his side. "You probably don't believe me—and I don't blame you if that's true—but I would never hurt you. When I found out that Edwin was arrested, it scared me. When I'm frightened, I shut down. I had to learn quickly that people take advantage of your emotional state, so I rarely show it, especially when something bad happens."

I nodded because I understood that all too well. Never let your guard down, even around the people you thought loved you the most. But with Knight, that was exactly what I did.

His hand slid up my neck and cupped my cheek. "When you came into my life, I did what I had learned: I built that wall. But you came up to the North Side with a pick in your hand and chipped away at everything you saw, including me. And now I'm crumbling around you, and I don't know what to do."

My heart thudded between my ears. He was asking for help. This was a guy who had everything he could ever want; he could pay anyone to do his bidding, yet he turned to me.

I slipped my hands around his waist and pulled him close. Knight was warm as I pressed my fingers against his flexing muscles. I wanted to hold him and never let him go.

"I'll help you. I know you're used to controlling things. Keeping things secret, but you have to open up to me."

"But you could get hurt."

I pulled back and gazed up into his sparkling gray eyes. "You forget where I'm from. I can take care of myself. I'm not your little sister. But I suspect she'll grow up tough too."

His lips twitched. "Yeah, sometimes I think she's tougher than me."

"You love her; that's why you're doing all this. But know that I'm here to help. We can fight together, Knight."

"Okay, then I better tell you what I know. I bailed Edwin out of jail and hired some people to protect him. I suspect my uncle is coming after him. I gave him the phone you got from that bus driver to see if he could find anything relating to my uncle on there. He called me the day before he was arrested and told me he found something, but it wasn't directly related to my uncle. I was going to meet with him after school, but then they arrested him."

I took his hand and guided him to the bed, where we sat on the edge.

"If he's out, have you had contact with him?"

"I'm meeting with him for lunch today."

"Okay. Great. Maybe we can find out what happened to the bus driver and who caused the brakes to fail."

"You can come with me, if you want."

A smile grew on my face as I was about to agree to go, but then I remembered. "I can't. I promised to go to Mrs. Hillingham's Pumpkin Luncheon."

He nodded as he took my hand in his. "Why are you still hanging out with Seraphina?"

"Like you, I want to learn the truth. And I think Seraphina's only being nice because she wants something from me. I thought it was so I wouldn't sue, but then I learned something at her birthday bash."

"What?"

"Her mom was from the South Side, like me. Even grew up in a trailer park. Not even Arabella knew that. There's something going on with Seraphina, and it involves her mom." I shrugged. "I don't know, but I get a weird vibe around her mom, like she's hiding something. She seems nice, but then I look at Seraphina and wonder, how could a sweet mom raise such a bitch?"

Knight turned, bringing his knee up on the bed to face me. "She was one of the investors in that drug I told you about. She was never nice to me when I was with Seraphina. She acted sweet in public, but if I went to Seraphina's house, she treated me like the help. Don't ever let her flattery fool you."

I tilted my head. "I'm not easily deceived, Knight. I'm not like Seraphina. If someone tells me I'm pretty, I wouldn't fall all over myself for them. Like I said, I get an odd vibe from her."

"That's not what I meant. You called her nice. The only time she has ever been nice to someone is to get something from them."

Pulling my hand from his, I said, "It's not like you were nice to me in the beginning either."

"Because I thought you were working

for my uncle. And when I was nice, there was a reason."

My mouth fell open, and I stood. "So, the only reason people are nice around here is to get something out of them?"

"Sometimes." He shrugged. "But I'm not like that anymore with you. After I realized you weren't helping my uncle, I decided I had to find out why my uncle wanted you around. But in the process, I started to like you. Then we fucked, and I really liked you after that." He wiggled his eyebrows.

I reached over and lightly slapped him on the shoulder. "You're the worst."

"I think you mispronounced 'best.'" He grabbed my hand and tugged me forward, causing me to fall on top of him.

We enjoyed the moment, laughing until our smiles faded. His eyes inspected my face. "I promise not to keep anything from you again. You're right. I need your help just as much as you need mine."

I stared into his uncertain gaze as he expected me to take his olive branch, and all the confusion melted away. I guessed I was waiting on the first crack in his hardened demeanor to catch a glimpse at what lay inside.

Knight was just a boy who felt the heft and gravity of responsibility for his sister, without the helpful hand of a parent to guide him. He was only sixteen when that terrible reality was thrust on him. Most people would fall apart under that pressure. My mom could barely handle me, and that boy was working hard to create a good, safe life for his sister.

Did he need help? Most definitely. But so did I.

"You're right. And once the sun comes up, we can help each other. Together."

He leaned over and kissed me. That was what we did for as long as I could remember. We even fell asleep with our lips barely touching. Just holding each other with that rare feeling that we were safe because we had each other.

TWENTY-ONE

Violet

I SCRUNCHED UP MY nose as I stared at myself in the mirror. "I'm not sure about this one. It seems a little glitzy."

"But it is gorg! Maybe a tad bit over the top for a luncheon, but I just wanted to see you in it," Arabella said as she stared at my reflection in the floor-length mirror.

"I like it," Knight added, staring at my ass.

I smirked, turning to face him. They both sat on a red loveseat against the wall.

We were in one of the spare bedrooms that had been used as a storage closet for his parents' things. Both Arabella and Knight agreed to help me pick out an outfit to wear to the Pumpkin Luncheon today.

After our talk in my bedroom early this morning, things between Knight and I have been good. More than good, amazing. We could barely keep our hands off each other. Except for now, when he couldn't stop looking at my ass.

"Are you sure it's okay if I wear your mom's clothes?" I asked, uneasy with him seeing me in her things.

"I wouldn't have brought it up if I wasn't okay with it. Besides, I was planning to donate her clothes anyway. If you want anything, take it. I have the things from my parents that actually meant something. A dress or sweater my mom wore once doesn't mean much to me."

I tilted my head. "Once? If I owned this dress, I'd wear it grocery shopping. I'd wear the hell out of it."

Arabella threw her head back and laughed. "I know what you mean. Your mom could have opened her own boutique with the amount of clothes she owned."

"She had a bit of a shopping problem. I loved my parents, but my mom wasn't perfect." Knight smiled, but as the moments passed, his grin slowly faded.

I stepped over to him, sitting on the arm of the loveseat. "I'm sure she would be proud of how you protected your sister from your uncle."

"I'm not doing this." He ran his fingers through his hair. "I'm not here to live in the past. I'm here to live in the present.

Here's something else that was my mom's that you can have." He got up and walked over to a small table. Pulling out a drawer, he reached inside and lifted a gold chain with a flower pendant hanging down the middle. The center was a yellow gem with dark blue gems making up the petals.

"Hey, it's a violet," Arabella noticed.

"Wow, that's beautiful. Are you sure you'll be okay with me borrowing it?" I got up and stepped over to Knight.

He lifted it and placed it around my neck. "No, not borrow. It's yours."

I gasped and cupped the jeweled flower in my hand. "That's too much, Knight. I'm not used to wearing something so nice—"

He traced his finger down the thin chain until he was cupping my hand. "Then you should get used to it. It's perfect for you. It's a violet. I mean, you can't get any more obvious than that. Even the color of the diamond and sapphires sets off your—"

"Diamond and sapphires?" My eyes widened as I pushed his hand away and lifted the pendent for further inspection.

"Yes. My mom wasn't about to wear fake jewelry. You've seen how many clothes she had. She was a big believer in 'go big or go home.'" He chuckled.

My palms became slick as I turned over the jeweled flower in my hand. My mom had given me the occasional cheap bracelet or gold-painted metal hoop earrings before, but nothing that cost her more than a few bucks.

I had never had something that cost this much in my hand before. I hadn't been this nervous since I was locked up a few weeks ago when I was accused of killing John Lenker.

"I don't think I can wear this. It's gorgeous, Knight, but what if I lose it?"

He shrugged. "Then you lose it. It's

yours to do what you like."

Knight turned and headed toward the door but stopped right before he got there. He lifted his phone from his pocket. "Oh shit."

"What's wrong?" I asked, looking up from studying the pendant.

"Have you seen this?" He walked over and shoved his phone at me. Arabella came and peeked over my shoulder.

I gasped, "That's the bus driver." I recognized his face in the photo.

"He's dead," Arabella said.

"Another body found in the school basement. What the hell?" My heart thudded in my chest.

"Poor Jewel. I wonder if she knows." Arabella looked up at me.

"I don't know. She might have already moved. I'll text her on my way to the luncheon to see what she says."

"I'll tell Edwin when I see him. I'll also beef up security around him," Knight said as I handed back his phone.

We all stood there in silence before Knight said, “I need something to drink. You two want anything? I’m heading to the kitchen.”

“Just water,” I said, and Arabella told him to make it two.

Knight turned and left.

“Can you believe that shit? This is getting so crazy,” Arabella pointed out.

“Let’s talk about anything but death. I’m kind of freaked out right now, and I really don’t want to be.”

“Right.” Arabella pointed to my necklace. “That necklace is amazing.”

I sighed. “Don’t you think it’s a little much?”

“Hell no. I swear if you don’t take it, I will.”

“I’ve never even held anything that had a real jewel in it before. Now Knight wants to give me this?”

“You know why, don’t you?”

I rolled my eyes. “No, of course I don’t. The only thing I can think of is he’s so rich that giving out diamonds and sapphires is like handing out candy for Halloween.”

Arabella snorted. “That’s probably true, but he gave you his mom’s necklace because that boy is in love. With you.”

I shook my head. “He likes me, but it’s not love. We had a good talk early this morning. I think it helped him get some things off his chest that had been bothering him. Maybe this was his way of saying thanks.”

She lifted her brow. “You two are perfect for each other. You both are in all sorts of denial.”

I waved her off. “Whatever. Let’s get back to clothes. I need to leave soon.”

“That’s right. And we still need to do your makeup and hair.” Arabella scurried across the room to another rack of clothes.

There were at least five racks of clothes that I could see. Some things were buried behind old furniture and even more racks.

"Hair and makeup. I'm not getting married," I joked.

"But you are going to a Pumpkin Luncheon. That may not be as big a deal as Seraphina's birthday bashes, but it's still significant. Think of Seraphina's birthday party as the party for the younger crowd—the teenagers and young adults. The Pumpkin Luncheon as the place to be for the older crowd."

I frowned. That sounded even less appealing than when I had to go to Seraphina's party.

"Ugh, so there's going to be mimosas and party games. Shit like that."

Arabella lifted a brown dress. "Perfect." Her eyes lit up as if she discovered the Holy Grail.

"It's brown."

There was nothing to it, just brown cloth. No pattern, no embroidery. I guess I didn't have the eye for fashion that

Arabella had because, in my opinion, it looked like a chocolate-colored potato sack.

"It's a wrap dress and with your new necklace, it's going to make that thing pop. And with its simplicity, your body will be what makes it wow people. Trust me."

I sighed. "I guess I must since you told me I need an entire makeover. I don't have time to disagree."

"Let's head to your bathroom. When we're done, Seraphina will be ready to sink her claws into you since she had to pay tens of thousands for something you were born with."

"What's that?" I asked as she took me by the hand and led me out of the room.

"Beauty, both inside and out. And a banging body."

We ran into Knight in the hallway where he gave us our drinks. She told him to stay away, and he'd see me when I was presentable.

He chuckled. "Good, I was getting bored with the clothes thing anyway. I'll be in my room. Grab me when you're about to leave."

Arabella didn't waste time as she made me over. After about thirty minutes, I put the dress on and looked at myself in the mirror.

"Holy shit. You were right. This dress is amazing. And my hair. Did you take hair styling lessons?"

My hair was up in a French twist with strands of hair falling around my face. It looked sophisticated but a little sexy too. And my makeup was flawless with a rosy lip stain that was beautiful.

"Damn. If I wasn't so short, I swear I could be a model," I said and puckered my lips, pretending I was on a catwalk in Paris.

"You're a work of art, bitch!" Arabella waved her hands around me with a grin.

"Ugh, and now I have to waste it on a bunch of oldies at some stupid luncheon."

"We'll go out later. Party it up." She elbowed me in my side.

I nodded, and we locked arms, heading out of my room.

Once we got to Knight's door, she knocked.

"Come in," he yelled.

"Presenting Violet Adler, a work of art," Arabella said with a giggle as she pushed open the door, shoving me in front of her.

Knight had been relaxing back on his bed, staring at his phone. When he turned his head, his eyes grew large.

"Uh, wow. You look . . ." he trailed off as he got up and came over to me. He traced the chain to where it dipped between my breasts. "You look incredible."

My breath hitched as he lowered his head, brushing my lips with his before dotting kisses on my chin and neck.

"I'm right here. And don't mess up her

makeup. I worked hard on that," Arabella reminded us that we weren't alone.

Knight let out a groan before standing straight.

"You did a superb job, but she's beautiful without it too." Knight's eyes sparkled as they dipped to my chest.

"Okay, sexy devil, I need to get Cinderella to the ball. She needs to go own that pumpkin."

I shook my head, and my heart fluttered as Arabella pulled away. "Bye, Knight. I'll see you after."

He nodded and waved. "I'll tell you what I learn from Edwin."

When Arabella helped me pick out a purse before we left the storage room, I wanted something big enough to hold my phone. Just in case Knight called with big news.

I grabbed the yellow leather shoulder bag, and we headed downstairs. Right as I opened the door, I heard Ava call for me.

I turned, and she had a small box in her hand. Gasping, I placed my hand on my chest. That was so sweet. She was giving me a present. That little girl was adorable.

"Oh, Ava. Is that for me?" I slid my eyes to Arabella, who was grinning too.

Bending down, I opened my palm.

"Yes." She pushed the velvet box in my hand.

I hoped she hadn't spent money on it. She was only six. I didn't think Knight would approve of her buying jewelry at such a young age.

"That's sweet, Ava. You didn't need to get me a gift—"

She scrunched up her adorable brows. "No, it's not a gift for you. I want you to take it back to Seraphina. Tell her we don't like it."

My grin faded, and I stood straight. "Oh, I see."

"Don't open it. Trust me. Just give it back to her since you're heading to her house. Tell her it's ugly." Ava turned and walked back toward the kitchen.

"I'd say it's the thought that counts, but that would make it worse." Arabella could barely get out her words as she laughed.

"Hey, I wouldn't be laughing too hard. You're just the coachman taking Cinderella to the ball."

She held up a finger. "Don't forget the fairy godmother too. Who do you think waved her wand and turned your rags into riches? Me, that's who."

I patted her on the back as we walked outside. "Then lead the way, fairy godmother. And take me to my fate."

TWENTY-TWO

Violet

I WAVED AT ARABELLA as she drove off. Glancing around, I couldn't help but notice no one was out front of the Hillingham's home.

When Seraphina had her party, there were valets and security, but there was nothing today. I hoped I was at the right location. Maybe the luncheon was being held in a hotel or restaurant?

I shuffled through my purse for the invitation and lifted it. Yup. This was the address.

I reached over to ring the doorbell when the door flew open. I gasped as I saw a slightly disheveled Crystal standing there with a look of surprise on her face.

"You're early," she said.

It was noon. I figured a luncheon would be at noon.

"I don't think so . . .." I glanced back at the invite in my hand. The fancy lettering read twelve o'clock, and I held it up for Crystal to see. "It says noon."

Crystal reached forward and grabbed it from my fingers. "Oh, no, you got the wrong invite. The printers. They screwed up the first batch, so I had them redo them. Your invite must be one of the old ones. It's supposed to be at two o'clock."

Shit. I was early.

I threw my thumb over my shoulder. "I could come back closer to that time."

"No, don't do that." She pursed her lips. "It was my fault for not double-checking those invitation baskets my assistant made. She's always making mistakes like that. Come inside. Maybe you could help with getting the luncheon ready."

I nodded and stepped past her as she moved aside.

"Yes. I'd be glad to help. Just let me know what you need me to do, and I'm on it." I smiled and glanced around.

I had never seen the front entrance. It reminded me of a grand entrance in an old Hollywood movie. There were two curved staircases that lined both walls with ornate wrought-iron railings.

At the end of the staircases were statues of women holding baskets. And the stairs and floor were a beautiful creamy marble.

"My goodness, Violet. You look lovely." She gazed down at my dress. When her eyes landed on my necklace, she flinched. "That necklace. It's simply stunning. And so perfect for you."

I nervously clasped the pendant in my hand. "It was Knight's mother's necklace. He gave it to me."

It was obvious she had seen it before. Perhaps his mother was wearing it the last time she saw it. It must have been hard for her to see me in it. I knew I shouldn't have worn it.

"I thought it looked familiar." She gazed up at me with shining eyes and a wide grin.

I glanced around. "Do you want me to

ask the kitchen staff if they need any help?"

She stepped forward, placing her arm around my shoulder. "Actually, there's something a little more delicate I need your help with. Something I can't trust the staff with, if you know what I mean." She winked.

A nervous giggle bubbled to the surface. It didn't matter that Crystal was from my part of town; she was just as snobbish as a lot of the other rich people I had encountered here.

I bet she wanted me to bring out an expensive vase that she didn't want the *help* to know about.

"It's in the basement. It's a room where I keep the things that need to stay locked up. Some personal items and expensive art, that sort of thing."

Of course. I tried not to roll my eyes.

She led me to a door behind one staircase and opened it. When she switched on the light, I saw it had stairs that led down to the basement.

"Just go down the stairs and make a right. It's the second door on the left."

I nodded. "What am I getting?"

A smile slowly broke out on her face, and the hairs on the back of my neck rose. "There's a cardboard box in the room's corner. It's filled with my mother-in-law's china dessert plates. They've been in the family for generations."

"No problem." I turned and stepped down.

"Oh, and Violet?"

I looked back. "Yes."

"Try to be careful. The box is heavy, and those plates are priceless."

"Of course." I forced a smile as she slowly closed the door.

There was something off about her today. I had a sense of dread, like that moment in horror movies when the young girl goes into the creepy basement alone at night. You knew she was about to be killed.

I felt like that stupid girl.

But I shouldn't. As I went down the stairs, I found the basement wasn't old and dingy; no, it was almost as posh as the upstairs. The only difference was there were wood floors down here instead of marble.

And the main area had couches and stuffed chairs with a large screen television on the wall. It felt like a nice family room. As I turned the corner of the stairs, I noticed a small kitchenette. It was nicer than the one I grew up with and bigger too. I guessed the Hillingham's weren't laminate counters and old, broken wood cabinets sort of people. No, this kitchenette boasted white marble counters and dark wooden cabinets.

For a moment I was jealous of Seraphina. That she grew up like this and probably never realized how good she had it.

But then my resentment died when I glanced at the wall. There was a mirror there, and I saw how I looked. Smiling, I touched the necklace Knight gave me and then reached up to the hair Arabella worked hard on.

I was beautiful, and it was thanks to my friends. The people who loved me. I thought about how Seraphina was pretty and all that made her so.

She was enhanced by things that cost money, not by love and friendship. Her enhancements came from makeup artists, hair stylists, and surgeries on her tits.

"I am a work of art. The kind love made," I whispered to myself.

Then something flashed in my head, and I sucked in a breath. I remembered something . . . a memory from before my mom died. That night we argued.

There were some moments from that night that were still foggy.

My mother loved my dad, and she kept insisting that he loved her too. Whether that was really true or not, at this moment, I was choosing to believe it was.

I wiped a lone tear that rolled down my cheek. "I miss you, Mom," I whispered.

Pushing my shoulders back, I moved forward. Now was not the time to feel sorry for myself. If I got the box for Mrs. Hillingham, then maybe I could hide out in the kitchen with the staff until the party. I'd be more comfortable around them.

"Second door on the left," I mumbled

as I found the door.

I frowned at the doorknob. There was a keyhole. Shit. It was probably locked since it was where she kept the expensive stuff. I reached for the knob anyway to check and found that it turned easily.

Shrugging, I opened the door and stepped inside. It looked like a storage room, and there wasn't even a window. I flipped on the light and saw it filled with small pieces of furniture and boxes. Lots of boxes.

Ugh. How many boxes was I supposed to open to find the damn plates? She said it was in the back corner, so I started at one corner.

I slid between the furniture and boxes as I made my way toward the back. As I did, my foot caught on something, and I tripped. I caught myself before I fell face first into a table, but my purse wasn't so lucky.

It hit the floor, and everything inside rolled out.

"Damn it." I got down on my hands and knees, searching for the lipstick Arabella insisted I take with me, my phone, and finally, that box Ava had given me.

I found everything but the box. Looking around, I lowered my head to the floor. I glimpsed it under a table. I reached over and pulled it out, noticing it had fallen open.

Thankfully, the chain was attached, and as I pulled, the necklace that was inside came along with it.

"What the fuck?" I said with a gasp as I held up the necklace. It was a tooth . . . an adult human tooth.

No wonder Ava didn't like it. What the hell was Seraphina into that she would give that to Knight?

My finger slid over the tooth, and a horrifying thought popped into my head. I shook my head and muttered "no" over and over again.

My tongue slid into the spot of my mouth that was missing a tooth. *Was that tooth mine?*

I glanced around the room. There had to be a mirror somewhere in here. What storage room doesn't have a discarded mirror?

That was when I saw a small wall mirror. It was wavy, like something I'd see in a girl's college dorm or a 90s sitcom.

I got up and slipped through the maze of boxes until I was in front of that mirror. I tugged back my lips and lifted the tooth. It looked like it would fit, and the coloring was the same.

When I pulled my lip back on the other

side of my mouth, I noticed it matched the tooth that mirrored its location.

That was my tooth. Seraphina made a necklace out of the tooth I lost in the bus accident. What sort of sick fuck did something like that?

I scrambled over to the box to see if there was anything else. I pulled out a piece of paper. It read: *Not only did you get the house you wanted, but you got your wish too. Violet is gone.*

I gasped and dropped the paper. Knight wanted me dead?

The door slammed shut, causing me to yelp. I got up and scurried over to the door but found it was locked. After pounding on the door a few times, I stopped and listened.

Nothing.

I banged again, but this time I heard something. It sounded like laughter.

"Help me. The door is locked!" I yelled.

"I know. That's why I closed the door, trash."

My skin pricked as I realized who was on the other side.

"Please, Seraphina. I know you think this is funny, but it's not. Let me out."

"Oh, see, my mom wouldn't like that very much. She's the one who told me to lock you in here."

Was that even true?

"First you try to kill me with the bus and now this?"

"No, I didn't try to kill you. I just made sure you were locked in that bus. It was my mom's idea to send you flying in a bus with no brakes."

I shook my head. That made little sense.

"If that's true, then why has she been so nice to me? She invited me here today."

She chuckled once more. “God, you really are a stupid bitch. You don’t belong here. You’re trash. You should be dead, but apparently you’re the cat with nine lives. But that ends tonight. Mom made sure of it. Don’t you even know?”

“Know what?”

“That she set all this up. She told me it’s easier to fool someone if you tell them you understand their pain. Always pander to people’s emotions. Works every time. Take their anger and hurt and act like you care, when in actuality, you don’t give a shit. Why do you think I was suddenly nice to you, bitch?”

My teeth ground together. I couldn’t believe I had been so gullible. I knew there was a reason she had been nice to me suddenly.

“You’re just mad because Knight is with me,” I screamed as tears trailed down my cheeks.

"*Please.* You can have him. You know he's just using you too. Who do you think first told me all about you? I mean, don't you think it's a little suspicious that he found you at Happy Pond in the middle of the night? Why was he there? Yet no one questioned him? That guy has a screw loose, and I wouldn't be surprised if he killed your mom. Probably feels guilty about it, so he gives you a few orgasms. That doesn't mean he loves you, Violet."

Every word she said made sense, and I hated her for it. I slid to the floor and let the tears flow.

"And if you haven't figured it out by now, because you really are that dumb, you're locked in here until you die. The only people who are allowed back here are me and Mom. Dad never goes into the basement, and the staff do as they're told.

Scream all you want, you'll die cold and alone, just like your mom."

"No," I bawled.

"My mom has plans. Big plans. Investments. And you are the one thing in the way of that. There's a special drug that will make her lots of money. Then we can finally get away from my father."

Was she talking about that failed cancer drug from Franklin First? Knight told me Crystal had been an investor once it failed.

"What drug?"

"Not that it matters to you since you'll be dead soon . . . but I guess there's no harm in letting it out since you don't know shit anyway. It's a good thing Jack Franklin died, and that cancer drug failed. My mom's friend had an idea to do something even better with the drug. Something that will make lots of money. But you came here and caused problems. Distracted the mayor for some reason. So, now you have to go. Bye-bye, bitch."

I heard her shoes click on the floor as she walked away. I sat there for a few moments sobbing before I realized I had my cell phone.

I got up, moved to the middle of the room while wiping the tears from my face. Grabbing my phone out of my purse, I tapped it.

Fuck. No signal.

I moved around the room holding it up, and at no point did I even get one bar. I went to the back wall, but nothing.

Seraphina was right. I was trapped with no way out.

I spent the next half hour tearing open boxes to find something to help, anything.

There was one last box, and my shoulders slumped, already knowing it wouldn't contain anything that would be of use.

When I ripped it open, my mouth fell. Lying right on top of photographs and paperwork was a picture.

She was young, close to my age, maybe a little older than me, with her arm around a man. He was handsome.

It was my mother, and she was pregnant.

She was staring up at him and looked like she was in love.

I flipped the picture over, and it had the year, confirming she was pregnant with me in the photograph.

He knew . . . He knew she was going to have a baby. I was both happy and heartbroken.

I squinted and noticed some writing. It had been smudged and was difficult to make out as it aged with time. I grabbed my phone and used my camera to magnify it.

I blinked as the realization settled on me. This man, tied to so much death, was my father. I choked out a sob as so many pieces fell together.

And now, I'd die in here, alone. All because of him.

About the Author

Josie Max is the second pen name for a USA Today Bestselling author. She's a passionate writer of dark heroes, twisted tales, and delicious love stories. Her other passions include reading and coffee. Obviously, she has no life. But that's good, because more time to think up wicked, dark romances with bullying men and fierce heroines. When she's not writing, she's rangling her two little boys and snuggling up with her husband at night so they can pass out from exhaustion together after putting the kids to bed.

www.josiemaxwrites.com

www.ingramcontent.com/pod-product-compliance
Lightning Source LLC
LaVergne TN
LVHW010052110826
845155LV00028B/299

* 9 7 8 1 9 5 5 1 8 4 0 1 4 *